"Lianna, I'm going to need you and Henry to come with me."

Go with him? She forced a caustic laugh out of her mouth even though she felt shaky with fear. What was he doing here? What was he playing at? "I'm not going anywhere with you."

"Your new guest isn't safe."

It sent a bolt of icy fear down her spine, but she refused to show it. "And you are?"

"I know you don't believe me, but yes. I am."

"I told you to go, Reece. If that's your name."

"It's my name."

"Sure."

"Lianna... The man who made this reservation... There's too much of a coincidence to the timing. I didn't find any listening devices outside, but maybe he overheard our conversation."

Lianna stilled. She had taken the listening device off the smoke alarm and shoved it into her desk drawer. Would whoever was listening know she'd tampered with it? Obviously. It would have changed what they could hear.

SUMMER STALKER

———

NICOLE HELM

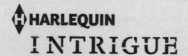

To back roads and the strange places you find on them
that inspire whole books.

HARLEQUIN®
INTRIGUE®

ISBN-13: 978-1-335-40173-1

Summer Stalker

Copyright © 2021 by Nicole Helm

Recycling programs
for this product may
not exist in your area.

This edition published by arrangement with Harlequin Books S.A.

For questions and comments about the quality of this book,
please contact us at CustomerService@Harlequin.com.

Harlequin Enterprises ULC
22 Adelaide St. West, 40th Floor
Toronto, Ontario M5H 4E3, Canada
www.Harlequin.com

Printed in U.S.A.

Nicole Helm grew up with her nose in a book and the dream of one day becoming a writer. Luckily, after a few failed career choices, she gets to follow that dream—writing down-to-earth contemporary romance and romantic suspense. From farmers to cowboys, Midwest to *the* West, Nicole writes stories about people finding themselves and finding love in the process. She lives in Missouri with her husband and two sons and dreams of someday owning a barn.

Books by Nicole Helm

Harlequin Intrigue

A North Star Novel Series

Summer Stalker

A Badlands Cops Novel

South Dakota Showdown
Covert Complication
Backcountry Escape
Isolated Threat
Badlands Beware
Close Range Christmas

Carsons & Delaneys: Battle Tested

Wyoming Cowboy Marine
Wyoming Cowboy Sniper
Wyoming Cowboy Ranger
Wyoming Cowboy Bodyguard

Visit the Author Profile page at Harlequin.com.

CAST OF CHARACTERS

Reece (Conrad) Montgomery—One of North Star Group's lead field operatives, sent to find out what Lianna Kade knows about her late husband's murder.

Lianna Kade—Bed-and-breakfast owner and mother, trying to rebuild her life after her husband was murdered and she discovered everything he told her was a lie.

Henry Kade—Lianna's seven-year-old son.

Todd Kade—Lianna's dead husband, just one of his many aliases.

Granger MacMillan—Former North Star Group leader. He hired Reece when he originally signed on.

Shay—Current head of North Star Group.

Sabrina Killian & Holden Parker—Lead field operatives with Reece who help in his missions when necessary.

Elsie Rogers & Betty—Support staff for North Star Group.

Prologue

Two years ago

Reece Montgomery had seen many a man injured. Shootings. Explosions. He'd watched men die before he'd grown into a man himself.

But there was something particularly poignant about Granger Macmillan—the man who'd taught Reece how to be a good one—being confined to a wheelchair and looking gaunt and weak.

Granger sat in said wheelchair in front of the entire body of North Star, a secret group set up for the sole purpose of taking down the Sons of the Badlands, a powerful gang who'd caused destruction and death across the whole of South Dakota.

Reece would know. His parents had been Sons groupies for several years before the state had permanently taken him away from them. They were probably both dead now, though Reece refused to look into the matter.

They'd been dead to him too many years to count.

Reece wouldn't say he blamed the Sons of the Badlands for his unfortunate childhood, or for being bounced from foster home to foster home, but he was determined to take them down all the same.

The fact that they, in collaboration with another organization of morally bankrupt men, had set a bomb off in the heart of the North Star headquarters ate away at Reece. Also, the fact that Granger had been shot in the midst of said explosion, leaving him weak even all these weeks later, felt like a particular failure.

Reece didn't know what exactly he'd failed. He'd been hurt in the blast himself, but was mostly healed now. He just knew…this wasn't right. Nothing that had gone down the day of the explosion was right.

Never mind the fact that, with some help, North Star had won—catching the man who'd left the bomb. Winning was so much less satisfying when he was in a room filled with the collateral damage from that victory.

"As you can see," Granger continued, "I'm not going to be physically capable of taking the reins back for quite some time." Even his voice sounded tired. Still, he was here and clearly determined to give the speech, and the room of about fifty field operatives, IT people and medical staff stayed very quiet in order to hear him.

"Shay will be my replacement until I'm able to return."

No one spoke a word. If there were concerns or doubts, no one voiced them. No one would dare. Even in a wheelchair, recovering from both a bullet wound and the injuries due to the blast, Granger Macmillan was their leader.

Shay could take over for a while—Reece figured she'd do well enough. She too had been hurt in the explosion—burns, mostly. She was recovering quickly, much like Reece and the others who'd been in the building and injured, but not shot like Granger had been.

Shay was a rarity in North Star. She'd lasted more than the prescribed four years. She had experience in each of North Star's many areas of expertise. No one could *replace* Granger, to Reece's way of thinking, but Shay could certainly step in and hold things together while he got his strength back.

If Reece had been thinking about it over the past year, he might have noticed Granger was grooming her to be his replacement. She was given missions in every aspect of North Star's operations. Granger sometimes asked her advice. Despite multiple instances where she hadn't followed orders, or even some where she'd gone directly against them, Shay was always a part of North Star. In retrospect, it was clear she was Granger's second-in-command, ready to take over at a moment's notice.

Reece had just never considered Granger bowing out or getting injured, or anyone *needing* to step in.

Shay took the floor next to Granger.

"You all know me well enough. I've been here longer than any person here except Granger himself. I hope you know, no matter what it may look like on the outside, I've always been dedicated to eradicating the Sons. Like most of you, they are responsible for the deaths of loved ones of my own. As acting temporary head of North Star, I can assure you we won't slow down or stop until our mission is done."

She looked down at Granger in his chair, something odd passing over her expression. Reece didn't know her well enough to figure it out.

"We won't quit now. Not when we've made real progress. I know some of you will balk at a new leader, but I hope you'll do me and Granger the courtesy of bringing it to me and letting us try to work it out. North Star will go on as it always has while Granger recovers. That I promise you."

Reece watched Granger's face. It was impassive. Something about that lack of expression or emotion, no matter how common for Granger, made Reece wonder if there really was a recovery expected—at least one that would bring him back to lead an elite group dedicated to taking down a gang as dangerous as the Sons.

"Our fight doesn't stop with one setback. As we all heal, we're going to keep working, keep fighting, and we'll make sure the Sons are wiped out forever."

There was some applause, some shouts of assent and encouragement. No one looked particularly defeated or upset about the change in leadership.

Because North Star had always been about one thing, and one thing only.

Wiping out the Sons.

Reece wouldn't stop until he'd helped bring that eventuality to fruition.

Chapter One

Present day

Reece was not a fan of meetings. He preferred for his duties to be communicated through one-on-one briefings or, even better, the written word. Still, with the Sons of the Badlands essentially decimated in every way that mattered to the North Star Group, Reece figured a meeting was necessary.

He arrived at the sprawling ranch house in eastern Wyoming that now acted as the headquarters of North Star. Though they had been moved in for well over a year, Reece still wasn't used to the change.

North Star was, in fact, his north star, orienting him and giving purpose to his life. He'd long ago given up hope of any kind of stability, but his work at North Star headquarters under the guidance of his mentor had started to get past the wall he'd built around himself, until the explosion two years ago. The blast had taken both from him—the headquarters, as well as the leader who had recruited him.

Granger Macmillan had retired. Reece still didn't know how to fully accept that a man he'd so respected had given up the fight for good and right and opted for…domesticity.

However, Shay was a fine enough leader. She was smart and firm like Granger, but she had her own ideas, and she implemented them as she saw fit. Reece didn't always agree, but he'd honed himself into a soldier long ago. He knew how to take an order.

And his mostly solo missions out in the field gave him the chance to go by his own internal sense of right and wrong.

Missions. They'd be over now, with the Sons of the Badlands completely and utterly annihilated. What little factions remained were of absolutely no consequence.

Now what will you do?

Reece didn't much want to figure that out, so he'd decided to go to this meeting and hope it wasn't about what he'd been dreading.

You're free to go, Reece Montgomery.

No one stayed in North Star for long. Even with Shay allowing people to stay beyond Granger's four-year rule, the explosion had cost them some good people who'd decided to move on. Since then, some others had left for law enforcement or other careers where they thought they could do more than grind the Sons of the Badlands into the South Dakota dust.

Now the Sons *were* dust, and what did that leave for North Star to do?

Holden Parker and Sabrina Killian were already sitting in Shay's office when Reece stepped in. They greeted each other with brief nods, and Reece took the lone empty seat.

Apparently, it would just be the four of them.

Shay didn't waste any time. She closed the door and stood in front of them, her expression grim and assessing.

"There isn't much left for us to do in our fight against the Sons of the Badlands," she said with no preamble, explaining what they all already knew. "There are still some very small, very ineffectual factions, but local law enforcement will be able to see to those without help from us."

"You disbanding us?" Holden Parker asked, legs thrust out and crossed at the ankles. He had his arms crossed casually behind his head, as though he didn't care.

But there wasn't anyone fooled in this room.

Everyone cared.

"Not as such," Shay replied evenly. "There are other groups. Other missions. If your personal mission ends with the Sons of the Badlands being reduced to rubble, then you're free to go. No questions asked."

"What's our other option?" Sabrina asked. She made no effort to appear casual. She leaned forward, fingers clasped tightly together, expression intense. As always.

Shay held up a small folder. "I've been approached by a small, secret group looking for help with a particularly difficult and sensitive mission. You three are here because I think you'd be the best options for the initial research and fieldwork. But it's only if you want to stay."

"What the hell else would we do?" Holden replied, his grin doing nothing to soften the bite in his voice.

Shay's gaze turned to Reece. He hadn't said a word—didn't make any effort to be casual or intense. If he allowed himself to consider it, he supposed the feeling that coursed through him was relief.

But he'd long ago given up *feeling*.

When Shay looked at him and simply *waited*, he gave a nod.

"I'm in," he said.

"Good, because you're up first. We have next to nothing to go on. A man was killed early last year, presumably via an unknown hit man. Because of this man's contacts and jobs, they believe there will be more targets. This organization doesn't know why. They don't know who. They barely know what."

"Don't make it so easy," Holden muttered.

But Reece was happy for complicated. For nearly impossible. It meant his life hadn't lost all purpose and meaning with the Sons eradicated.

He still had a mission to complete, and the more difficult the better.

"What we do have to go on is the widow. The government agency thinks she knows something, but she's been wholly unwilling to talk to them. Presumably, she blames her husband's death on his work, whoever his employers were. At this point, they're hoping a stranger and an uninvolved group like ours can get through to her."

"You going to tell us this agency's name?" Sabrina demanded.

Shay shook her head. "No. They've made it very clear everything is on a need-to-know basis, and knowing who *they* are isn't necessary."

"Then how do we know they're the good guys?" Reece asked.

"We don't," Shay said. "But they didn't ask me to get through to this widow via any means necessary. They didn't act as though they'd used any scare tactics. It could be for any reason, but it makes me more prone to want to look into this. They're not hurting or threatening an innocent woman, when they probably could be."

Her honesty was one of the things that Reece figured made her an excellent successor to Granger. Like Granger, she didn't let anyone labor under false pretenses. It was what had always made North Star work: knowing that a mission wasn't safe or easy. An agent was risking a lot.

"But we don't know for sure, obviously. That's part of what I want you to find out, Reece. I want you to pose as a guest at the widow's bed-and-breakfast. Find out what you can about what she might know, and the organization her husband was working for. We don't move forward with the rest of it until we get a better picture of who we're dealing with. I'll continue to research on my end, but I think the widow is the key to figuring out if we want to be involved. You'll do your best to befriend the widow and get whatever information you can."

Sabrina laughed. "Reece? *Befriend* someone? You've got to be kidding me."

Shay gave him what passed for a smile. "I'm sure he can handle it."

All Reece did was take the folder and nod.

HE COULD INDEED handle it. Truth be told, he knew how to turn on the charm when needed. Most especially when he wasn't himself. When he checked into the inn, he would be Reece Conrad, traveling nature photographer.

Reece knew how to play a role.

The Bluebird Bed & Breakfast was situated in eastern Wyoming, in the small town of Echo. As far as Reece could see, there was nothing special about the town except that it was nestled near the borders of both Montana and South Dakota.

It was a picturesque enough area. There were slight rolling hills as he drove along, with pretty ranches tucked away just off the two-lane highway. He passed the occasional rock formation—though nothing as grand as Devil's Tower a ways to the southwest.

Reece turned off the highway onto the paved but poorly maintained road mentioned in the directions on the Bluebird Bed & Breakfast's website.

It was a good half mile before he rounded a curve around a small pond and the house came into view. Reece slowed without fully realizing he was doing so.

The house and yard that came into view was like something out of a Norman Rockwell painting. The pretty little farmhouse looked just like the picture he'd seen on the website, with its gleaming white-and-blue shutters and an expansive porch with colorful chairs. Trees closed in around the house on three sides, but the front yard was sprawling and well kept.

It was like some stupid childhood dream he'd had of the perfect life. A family, a house like that and space to run.

He shook his head. He had to leave Reece Montgomery behind. He was Reece Conrad. A married man, two kids. He traveled from national park to national park via back roads, photographing landscapes and the various nature he found. He stayed at places off the beaten path, hoping for great pictures along the way. He was a man who'd had a normal childhood, gone to college and built a life.

He stopped the car next to a compact sedan. It was an older model, but it looked like it was kept in meticulous shape. Still, when he glanced inside the car, there was the debris of children in the back seat.

Though it looked to be the mess of more than one child, this was the make and model of Lianna Kade's car, according to the file he'd been given.

The proprietress, the widow, had one child. A son. Seven years old. That Reece knew from what Shay had been able to dig up on her. Mrs. Kade didn't have anything remarkable in her background. The house had been in her family since it was built, but it was her great-grandmother who'd turned it into a bed-and-breakfast in the late 1940s, after her husband had died in World War II.

The current innkeeper had married Todd Kade

when she was just twenty. Todd Kade wasn't his real name, but it was interesting that the widow had kept the last name for herself and her son.

Shay was still trying to track down the man's real name. If the agency wanting more information on his death knew, they weren't telling.

Reece hefted his duffel bag over one shoulder, and the camera bag meant to keep up pretenses over the other. He walked across the green yard. There were gardens…everywhere. Along the tree line, huge beds—protected by chicken wire—boasted what appeared to be local grasses. There were artful groupings of red and orange tulips and yellow daffodils. Bracketing the house and porch were more beds, pots and planters, full of flowers he was more familiar with. Pansies and impatiens and the like.

Reece made his way up to the porch. Hanging from the railing on one side was a cheerfully painted sign that said *Welcome to the Bluebird Bed & Breakfast*. There were little bluebirds painted around the words. Underneath was a tab that said *Vacancies*.

He took the stairs onto the porch. There was a welcome mat, more bluebirds. The door itself was painted a bright blue. The knob was an ornate metal that had been fashioned to look like a bird, as well.

He was fairly certain that if someone looked up *domestic bliss* in the dictionary, they'd find a picture of the Bluebird Bed & Breakfast.

Not that he knew *anything* about domestic bliss.

The directions he'd been given upon reserving a room had been to let himself into the house. Not very safe for a woman whose husband had been murdered just last year.

Still, Reece pushed the door open and stepped into what appeared to be a living room. A bell on the door tinkled, and he heard footsteps from somewhere deeper in the house.

A woman, blond hair pulled back in a swinging ponytail, entered the room. Her smile was warm and welcoming, though her blue eyes didn't quite match the expression. There was nothing particularly remarkable about her—she was medium height, medium build. She wore well-worn jeans and a T-shirt that had the name of the bed-and-breakfast emblazoned across the pocket.

Reece felt a bit like he'd had the wind knocked out of him, and couldn't begin to imagine why.

"You must be Mr. Conrad," she said, her voice polite and husky. "Welcome."

Okay, maybe Reece Conrad *wasn't* married with two kids. Maybe he was a very single man and—

He cleared his throat, not sure where all that... response came from. Or why he was oddly uncomfortable with the fake part of his name. "Please call me Reece."

"Of course. You can set your bags down if you like, and we'll get you checked in." She moved behind a desk, set up in a little alcove surrounded by windows that looked out over the front yard.

She carried the scent of lemons as she passed him.

"You're the...owner."

He noticed the infinitesimal stiffening of her spine, but her expression was perfectly friendly. "Yes, I am."

She jiggled the mouse of her computer, the monitor coming to life. She typed in a few things, then unlocked a drawer and pulled out a large envelope.

"You booked our attic room. You can follow me and I'll show you up, giving you a bit of a tour along the way."

"Sure."

She made a move to take his bags, but he grabbed them first. She didn't comment or slide him a look. She just started…talking.

"This is our common area. Cold nights—and we can have those well into June—we have a fire in the hearth. Through that entryway, you'll find the dining room and kitchen. On this side of the house you'll find the TV room. There's also a public computer you're free to use."

She led him to a staircase and Reece found himself unduly mesmerized by the swing of her ponytail.

Get a hold of yourself, Montgomery.

"This is the second floor. It's all guest rooms. You're the only guest here for right now, but this weekend we'll have an almost full house. Obviously we ask that you stick to your own room or the common areas downstairs."

"Of course."

She led him to a door and pulled a keychain out of her pocket. She fiddled through the keys until she found an antique-looking metal one. She fitted it into the keyhole and unlocked the door.

It pushed open with a creak. "You have a key in here," she said, shaking the envelope in her hand. "The staircase leads straight into the room, so I advise locking it when you want complete privacy. Cleaning hours are outlined in the packet in the envelope, and most guests are incredibly polite, but you just never know when someone might want to poke around."

She led him up a rickety staircase. He followed, half expecting the attic room to be, in fact, very attic-like.

"I read the history on your website," he offered, testing the friendliness waters. "It's always been in your family?"

"Yes, since it was built in 1900 by my great-great-grandfather. But it wasn't turned into a bed-and-breakfast until the 1940s by my great-grandmother. Nevertheless, much of the history you'll find here is related to my family."

"But your name is Kade, not Young."

She stopped somewhat abruptly on the stairs, then turned to face him. "It is. Did you have a personal question you wanted to ask about that?"

She reminded him of a very stern schoolteacher. "No, ma'am."

She nodded firmly and turned on a heel, and then finished the ascent up the stairs. He followed, giving her a respectable distance.

The room was the complete opposite of the narrow, creaky staircase. It was A-framed, with low ceilings on either side, but the bed was situated right in the middle of the room against the far wall. There were large stained glass windows on either side of the bed, big picture windows on the other walls that let in streams of light so that the whole room seemed to glow.

There was a desk on one side of the room, and a door on the other.

"The door leads to a small bathroom, but it's all yours. There's also a bathroom on the main level available to any guests. Breakfast is served from eight to nine in the dining room. We offer a small selection for a help-yourself lunch at noon. Dinner is from five to six. If you need to eat earlier or later, you can make arrangements."

"This is amazing."

"I'm glad you think so." She handed him the envelope and Reece noted the careful way she made sure her hands were nowhere near his when he took it. "Please enjoy your stay, and don't hesitate to ask for anything you might need. I'll do my best to accommodate."

"Thank you, Mrs. Kade."

She clasped her hands together and offered him a smile that, if he wasn't totally off base, had chilled considerably. "Please call me Lianna." She pointed to a phone on the desk. "Dial one if you need assistance."

With that, she turned and left the room. He heard the subtle *click* of the lock being engaged once she'd reached the bottom of the stairs.

Reece shook out the contents of the envelope she'd handed him. A pamphlet of information about the inn, a printout of events around town for the month and the key to his room door.

The top of the key was in the shape of a bluebird. Reece had never considered himself a fan of whimsy, but something about it made him smile.

But that smile only lasted a few seconds before he got to work.

In less than five minutes, he'd unpacked his clothes, found a secure place for his weapons and unearthed a listening device on the smoke detector.

Now the question was—who had put it there? Lianna Kade? The group who'd hired North Star?

Or someone else altogether?

Chapter Two

Lianna Kade was not one to make a mountain out of a molehill. She'd survived six years married to a man who'd shown himself to be a monster more and more over time. Then, once he'd been killed, she'd found out he was some kind of spy. All of that had given her the space to learn to handle what came, without getting too worked up about it.

But Reece Conrad was *something*. He made her... itchy, she thought as she walked down the attic stairs. She locked the door, making sure not to give one last look up the stairs.

It wasn't nerves so much. Though he was a quietly intense man, he didn't give off any kind of threatening vibe. She might have been very stupid and naive at twenty, but she'd honed those instincts she'd lacked then.

Reece Conrad wasn't a threat exactly, but she was tempted to call Sheriff Reynolds and see if he could run some kind of background check.

But that would only start the whole *thing* over.

Grandma had retired and handed over the bed-and-breakfast to Lianna to give her and Henry a fresh start. Away from everything that had happened.

Lianna had taken it because her grandparents and parents didn't know the half of what had *actually* happened, and she wanted to always keep it that way. They could stay off in Denver, and she could raise and support her son in one of her favorite places in the world.

The alarm on her phone went off. Time to walk up to pick Henry up at the bus stop. Time to get her head back into the important parts of her routine.

She went out the front door, telling herself to enjoy the walk on a pretty, late-spring day. So pretty that once she reached the parking lot, she glanced back at the house.

Perfect. A dream come to life, and she got to run it. Inn-keeping wasn't some perfect dream job, but living here… It was exactly what she wanted.

She happened to look up at the attic windows. Her stomach swooped in a jolt of surprise and embarrassment. Reece was standing there. Looking at her.

She turned quickly, striding for the road. She didn't look back. If he was watching her, well, so be it. She'd probably watch *him* if the situations were reversed.

She didn't usually have to worry about men in a suitable age range showing up at her B and B looking like…that.

Yes, situations reversed, she would look and she would indeed watch him walk away.

"You're hopeless, Lianna," she muttered to herself, forgetting her usual routine. Her walk up to the bus stop was supposed to be a meditative time. Resetting. Her therapist back in Denver had given her a lot of strategies for coping with her newfound anxiety.

He had *not* been supportive of the move to middle-of-nowhere Wyoming, even if it was home. But Lianna had needed this fresh start. For her. For Henry. She'd needed home, and a place to find her confidence.

She would have never done that in San Francisco, with all the lies Todd had told. All the lies that had ended up with him murdered. Not that anyone knew *why*. No, the story the papers had told had been a burglary gone wrong.

Lianna knew better. Six years too late, but she knew better. And no matter the horror those years with Todd had been, she'd gotten Henry out of them. She couldn't wish them away. Not when Henry was her whole world.

She'd moved here for him, too. Getting out of San Francisco and to Denver had been the first step. Her parents had gotten their lives together—after letting Lianna's grandparents raise her—and in the first months after the murder, they, along with her grandparents, had been rocks, standing solidly behind her. They had been everything she needed.

But now she needed space. She needed to do some things for herself without being afraid of her own shadow. Besides, when she ran an inn, no one cared how often she checked the locks.

Henry had been able to go to first grade in the same elementary school she'd gone to. He would grow up in the same town, in the same place she had. That was important. It was *right*.

She'd been afraid Todd's cronies at his little spy group would follow her here, forever harassing her for information. Forever so sure she knew more than she'd let on.

But she knew *nothing* about Todd, it turned out. She'd have to live with that for the rest of her life.

Once she'd moved out of Denver, they'd let her be. Thank God. She could relax. Enjoy her life. Far away from the lies and wrongdoings of her late husband.

Lianna stopped at the edge of the road where the bus would stop and let Henry off. She shaded her eyes against the sun as the bus rumbled around the curve. The door opened and Henry bounded off, already talking a mile a minute.

"Mom! Mom! Joey is getting a dog! Can we get a dog? Wouldn't it be great to have a dog?"

Lianna waved at the bus driver before turning to follow Henry back down to the house. "You're allergic to dogs."

Henry sighed heavily. "That's so stupid."

"I know. Terribly stupid. We could always try getting the shots."

Henry pulled a face. "I *hate* shots."

"I know." She slid her hand over his shoulder, giving her seven-year-old a squeeze. Truth be told, she was secretly relieved there was an excuse not to get a dog. Between Henry and the Bluebird, she didn't have the time or energy to take care of another living thing.

Not that it stopped her from feeling guilty over Henry's lack of pets.

"Can we get a bird?"

Lianna had to suppress the shudder that ran through her. "Well, maybe we can look into it." She might lean into the bluebird part of her bed-and-breakfast's name, but that didn't mean she actually wanted a bird in her *house*. Birds were best kept as artistic decoration.

"Or a lizard? Or a hamster? Maybe a ferret."

"We can talk it over more tonight. We have a guest today." *Never a ferret. Never.*

"It's not another old lady, is it?"

"Henry Patrick Kade."

"Well! They always smell like a bathroom. And that one pinched my cheek *every* time she saw me."

"The horror," Lianna replied dryly.

Henry raced ahead, then back to her, pretending to be an airplane. He made explosion sounds and at one point even somersaulted over the soft grass.

She should admonish him, since he'd forgotten to zip his backpack and a few papers and pencils fluttered out, as well as his water bottle jostling out of its side pocket. But it was almost summer and her baby was happy.

How could she scold that?

She picked up after him as he continued to expend the pent-up energy of a first grader who'd been stuck in school on a sunny day.

They began to cross the yard. Lianna had almost forgotten about Reece and the churning of…too many feelings at the sight of him. But he was standing on her porch, still as a statue, and she came to an abrupt halt.

He looked imposing. She felt the brief need to shield Henry from him, but that was silly. She knew how to take care of herself these days. Keep both her and Henry safe from anyone who might wish them harm.

Which was no one. She'd made it clear she knew nothing about Todd's death, understood nothing about whatever he'd been secretly involved in. She'd worked with the police and FBI and in the end had moved to a different state. She'd moved *home* to hunker down into the B and B.

Henry darted around her, clearly intrigued by the impressive-looking stranger. They didn't get a lot of guests under the age of seventy. "Hi, mister. Do you like birds?"

Reece's blank expression scrunched into something closer to befuddlement. "Uh."

"We're discussing the merits of different pets," Lianna offered, forcing herself to move forward. To act casually. She and Henry were safe. The police had assured her.

"Oh, well, I'd prefer a dog, I suppose."

"Ugh," Henry groaned. "Everything is stupid." He stomped up the stairs and slammed inside.

Reece gave a puzzled glance at the front door and then back at Lianna. "I'm sorry."

She forced a kind smile. "Don't apologize. He's having a bit of a crisis over being allergic to dogs."

"Ah."

Lianna pressed her lips together. Reece still seemed

utterly confused. "You don't have any kids of your own, do you?"

"No. Can't say I know much about kids."

"Everything being stupid is par for the course. In the next moment, he'll be happy as a clam thinking about something else."

"Well. Good. I just wanted to walk around and take some pictures, if you don't mind." He held up his camera.

"Of course. Be careful in the woods. It's easy to get turned around and you don't want to get lost."

"I think I'll be all right. Thanks." He walked off toward her gardens and snapped a few pictures as she watched.

There was something…*something*. But she had homework to oversee and dinner to make, and she didn't have time for *something*.

BEING THE LONE guest in an inn run by an attractive woman and her precocious son was… Reece really didn't know what it was.

He usually had no problems pretending to be someone else. He was in no hurry to be himself. But there was something so domestic about eating breakfasts and dinners with her and the kid. Watching Lianna walk Henry to the bus stop and back.

It was fascinating. He'd never witnessed that level of care or affection.

Which was not what he was here for.

He'd found five more listening devices scattered around Bluebird's common areas. At night, he'd sneaked into the other guest rooms and found one in each of those. He had yet to figure out how to get into Lianna and Henry's private area of the house without detection. Lianna struck him as the type of woman who'd know if the order of things had been disrupted. Besides, he'd seen a serious-looking security camera bolted above the door to her private quarters.

That being said, she didn't appear to be particularly nervous or careful. She was certainly somewhat suspicious of him, but every day he went out and took pictures, sometimes even showing the better ones to Lianna or Henry. Henry liked the pictures of animals he'd found, and Lianna asked him more technical questions about the camera.

He was never sure if she was interested or if it was a test.

More guests would be coming tomorrow, and he was no closer to having a clue how to unearth the necessary information than he had been when he'd arrived.

He took his usual afternoon walk, deep into the woods and away from sight or hearing distance to the house. Once he felt he was far enough away, he set up his computer and phone so he could make the phone call to headquarters.

He attached everything, connected to the secure server and dialed. Shay didn't bother with greetings.

"Anything?" she asked.

"Not really. I found a listening device in every room—not just the common areas, but all the guest rooms, as well."

"What about hers?"

Reece bit back a sigh. "I haven't had a chance to get into her private living space yet, but it's not her."

There was a pause. "Have you been *trying* to get into her rooms?"

"She's on the premises all the time. If I'm keeping my cover, I can't sneak into her room unless there's zero chance of being caught. She's clean, Shay."

"If you sent off one of the devices, we could run the diagnostics, maybe get a clue where it came from."

"Taking one of the devices poses a problem since we don't know who's placed them in the first place. If they know someone is on to them, it could escalate something. She and the kid shouldn't be caught in the cross fire of that."

"You have to get into her room and see if she's got them there, too. It's the only way to know for sure she's not involved."

Reece sighed. "She really takes care of this place—it's a family business. These kinds of listening devices in guest rooms would violate all sorts of privacy laws, not to mention they're way more high-tech than the cameras she has guarding her private quarters. I can't see her doing it. None of it would add up."

"But you don't know for sure she's not involved with the people doing it until you check her rooms. I trust your instincts, Reece, but we can't be too careful. We just don't know enough, and that's why I sent you. To *find out*. Now, I can ask this group hiring us if they're the ones who put the devices in."

Reece could read the hesitation in Shay's tone.

"No, I'd like to figure it out as much as I can on my own. We want to keep the widow and the kid out of it, don't we? That's a priority for me. Kids don't get caught in the cross fire."

"That's a priority for me, too," Shay returned.

"Do we have a time limit on this?"

"They haven't prescribed one, and I figure as long as nothing pressing is going on, you've got the time to earn the widow's trust."

Reece glanced back at the house. Earning Lianna's confidence was getting complicated. He figured it was the kid. He'd follow orders to complete a mission as long as it didn't interfere with his one simple moral tenet. *Don't get kids caught in the middle.*

He'd never had a mission—in the military or with North Star—where he'd had to deal with kids. This was a first, and he didn't like it.

"Reece?"

"It seems pretty peaceful here. Maybe it's the wrong line to tug to get the information."

"I might agree with you if you hadn't found listening devices."

Shay was right. The devices could mean Lianna and Henry were in danger and Lianna didn't have a clue. But despite a few days of being underfoot, Reece still didn't know how to bring up the subject of the dead husband and who he'd worked for. With no direct threat to her, it felt like bringing unnecessary trouble to her doorstep.

"Get into her rooms, Reece. Whether she knows what's going on or not, she might have something in her private quarters to point us in the right direction. We have to explore every possibility until we have more to go on."

Reece grimaced. He wasn't sure how he was going to accomplish that task, let alone how he'd live with the guilt of poking around in her private belongings when he did.

"All right, I—"

"Hey, Reece! Whatcha doing way out here?" Reece whirled on Henry, who was bounding through the trees.

Reece swore inwardly and slapped the phone and laptop shut. "Hey there, Hank," he said, trying to use his body to block the kid's view of the equipment.

Henry laughed like he always did when Reece called him Hank. Something shifted deep inside Reece, but he ignored it and shoved his laptop into his bag. There'd be no way of hiding it completely, but he could pretend it had something to do with the camera.

"I thought you weren't supposed to come out this far," Reece said as Henry came up on his side.

"I'm not, but I heard your voice." Henry peered at the bag. "Who you talking to?"

"Oh, I…got a call from my boss."

"Mom said her cell phone doesn't work all the way out here. Who's your boss?"

"Uh. The person who pays me to take pictures."

"That's cool. I think I want to be a firefighter when I grow up. My friend Joey's dad is a cop and he said firemen get to play video games all day."

"Huh. Well…"

Henry jumped up and down, trying to grab a tree

branch, presumably to hang off, but it was just out of reach. "But Mom says it's a dangerous job."

"That's…"

"I could help Mom with the inn, but it gets kinda boring way out here."

Reece smiled against his will. "Well, you probably have some time to figure it out."

Henry shrugged, giving up his attempt to jump and grab the branch. "Did you see any animals today?"

"No, not today."

"My other friend Avery has a dad who's in the army. It sounds pretty cool, but sometimes he goes away for a long time."

Reece was surprised at the viscerally negative reaction he had to that. Even more surprised when words tumbled out of his mouth. "I was in the military for a little while. It's not bad, but… Well, I think your mom would miss you. You have to travel a lot. Work and live overseas." *See things you can't unsee.*

"Have you been to foreign countries?"

"Yeah."

"Which one's the best?"

"Too many…to name."

"Did you ever get hurt?"

"A little."

Henry hopped again, though this time it seemed to be to some inner rhythm rather than trying to grab the branch. "How? Why? Where?"

"That's probably more of a bedtime story," Reece offered, hoping that would get him off this line of questioning.

"Will you tell it to me at bedtime, then? Mom usually makes me read." Henry rolled his eyes. "But sometimes she'll read to me. Maybe you could tell me the story instead."

"Well… I guess that would be up to her." It'd give Reece a reason to be in Henry's room. He doubted very much Lianna would leave them alone, but he could get an idea of the layout, maybe a way to sneak in when Lianna was busy with guests this weekend.

If she'd let him. "We should get you back. Your mom might worry."

"Can I carry your camera?"

"Sure. Sure." Reece handed it over.

And felt like slime.

Chapter Three

"You know we don't allow guests in our rooms, Henry," Lianna said, trying to add groceries to her online cart and give Henry her full attention. But he was going on and on about Reece, and she had dinner to start and groceries to order for the weekend. "It's a very important rule."

Henry's groan could have been heard in Montana. "He's my friend."

Pain cracked through Lianna's chest. Friend. A guest couldn't be a friend. Still, it was no mystery why he was fascinated with Reece. The man was the embodiment of adult male attention that Henry didn't get. That he'd never gotten, because Todd had not been a good father. He'd considered children the domain of the wife.

A complication.

Lianna had gone out of her way to shield Henry from that, but she couldn't make up for the lack. She knew... She knew what it was like to grow up without parents. No matter how much she'd loved her grandparents, knowing her parents couldn't take care of her had been... It was a scar. Even having them in her life now didn't change the fact that they hadn't been then.

Now Henry had his own scar and wanted some random stranger to tell him a bedtime story.

"It isn't fair," Henry said, turning a furious shade of red.

Lianna turned away from the computer. She'd found one person in town who would pick up and deliver for her, and the extra money was worth the time she saved. But Freya could only deliver on Saturday mornings, which *wasn't* convenient.

Neither was this. She forced a smile for her son. She would never let him know his feelings came at an inconvenient time. He would never ever feel like an inconvenience to her. "I'm sure he can tell you the same story in the common areas."

"I hate the common areas and this stupid place. I want to live in town like Joey. I want…"

He didn't say it, but she knew what he wanted. A father. She knew because everything in him wilted, the anger fizzling out. He could want a father with everything he was, but it couldn't make his father alive.

"I want to show him my map," Henry said, speaking of the wallpaper on one wall of his room—a map of the whole world. "He's been to foreign countries," Henry said loftily. Some of his anger had faded, but he hadn't given up the fight.

Lianna's chest still hurt, but she figured the hardest part of Henry's outburst was over. She turned her attention back to groceries. "Oh, has he?"

"Yeah, when he was in the military. He even got hurt."

Lianna's body went cold. Military. Todd hadn't been military, and neither had the group he'd been involved with, as far as she knew. Still, military was a far cry from unassuming nature photographer.

Military meant…guns. It meant knowing how to do things. Bad things. Scary things. It meant he wasn't so unassuming. It meant he wasn't safe. They weren't safe.

"Excuse me, Henry." She pushed away from the kitchen table and marched through the dining room, panic beating through her chest. She knew she had to control it before she talked to Reece. She had to—

But he was walking in the front door, carrying that backpack that was abnormally large for a camera. Wasn't it? Wasn't everything about him just a shade wrong?

You're being paranoid. This is what Dr. Winston warned you about. Being alone. Spiraling out of control.

"You were in the military." She blurted it out like an accusation and then winced at how off-balanced she sounded.

Reece didn't move a muscle. He simply stood in the entryway, eyebrows raised. "Yes," he agreed very calmly.

"I…I don't like people lying to me. To my son." Her throat felt too tight, anxiety cutting off the oxygen.

It's just in your head. Breathe.

"Lianna, I haven't been active duty for over five years."

And he wasn't *her* friend, or anyone but a guest in her inn. It wasn't his fault Henry was getting attached. It wasn't *a lie*… "If you want to stay longer, I'm going to have to run a background check on you."

He didn't pause or hesitate. "Okay."

She wanted to cry, and she didn't have the slightest clue as to why. Except she still wasn't right. She still wasn't herself. "I'm sorry."

"For what?" He didn't step toward her. He didn't do a thing but stand there. But his next words were so gentle it felt like he put a warm hand on her shoulder like her grandmother used to do when Lianna was unreasonably upset.

"You should always trust your gut, and you should always be careful to protect your son. Run whatever checks you need to feel safe. You should feel safe."

It was all she wanted. For her and Henry. "My husband was killed. Murdered." The words had fallen out. Words she hadn't spoken since they'd moved to Echo. Oh, she knew some people knew. Especially those who had been friends of her grandparents, but she hadn't had to say it.

Why had she said it now?

Reece blinked. "I'm sorry."

He didn't sound shocked or dismayed. His sorry was…kind, but not particularly effusive. She appreciated that. She hadn't wanted his gasp of horror or praise of her bravery. She only wanted him to understand.

"My husband wasn't who he said he was." She

swallowed and glanced back at the kitchen. Henry hadn't followed her. He was likely sneaking chocolate chips in the kitchen.

Thank God.

"Henry likes you. He's never had someone… Even when his father was alive, he didn't spend much time with Henry. He's desperate for… He likes you, and I…"

"I like him, too."

"You're just a guest. You…" She stepped forward. She couldn't explain it to Henry. He was only seven. But maybe if she explained it to this man, he could understand. He could…do something. "He can't get attached like that. I'm sorry. It isn't healthy. You won't stay forever."

"People generally don't."

Sadness dripped from those words. A sadness she recognized, because she'd been lost in it herself once. Henry had saved her, though. She'd had to take care of him, protect him, love him, and in doing all of those things for her precious boy, she'd learned to do the same for herself.

She wasn't perfect. Clearly this little meltdown wasn't at all mentally healthy. But Reece was just a person. With his own story. His own sadness and hang-ups. And he'd been here a few days and nothing out of the ordinary had happened. No questions about Todd. Nothing out of place. It wasn't like Denver.

She had to get a hold of herself. "I'm perfectly happy to let him hear your stories. A friendship is certainly acceptable, but you cannot come into our private quarters. I have to maintain that boundary."

The sadness didn't lift. If anything, he looked sadder. But he nodded. "Whatever you want, Lianna. He's your son." He held up his camera. "If you'll excuse me."

Then he left again, as if he hadn't come inside for anything at all. Somehow, despite him being a stranger, Lianna felt guilty about his feelings. Feelings she didn't understand.

And are none of your business.

But she stood, staring at the door much longer than a busy woman had any right to.

"YOU'VE GOT A fake background ready for Reece Conrad?" Reece demanded when Shay answered his phone call.

Shay didn't hesitate at his sudden phone call or the demand. "More or less."

"Make it airtight."

"Will do. She's suspicious?"

"Not exactly, but the kid… He likes me. God knows why. She's more worried about that sort of thing. She told me her husband wasn't who he said he was."

"So she knew he was shady."

Reece sighed. "Found out, anyway. Which isn't surprising. He *was* murdered."

"All the reports on it say it was a burglary gone wrong. And use the fake name. I bet she knows the real one. Did you—"

"I don't have any other updates," Reece bit out. "I just want to make sure the background is in place."

"It is, but we'll flesh a few things out if we know

she's running a check. Got a preferred wife name that you'll remember?"

"No wife."

"I thought…"

"She's seen me with the kid—she already called it that I don't have one of those. I haven't been wearing a ring, and I haven't mentioned a wife waiting for me. It doesn't make sense. Especially if I'm going to stay longer."

There was a long silence. "She's pretty," Shay said at length.

Reece didn't speak. No answer was better than anything he could have responded with.

Shay sighed. "All right. You'll look good for a background check—Elsie will make sure of it. If your innkeeper found out her husband wasn't who he said he was, she knows *something*." Shay's voice changed. Got hard and authoritative. "Get in her room, Montgomery. No more excuses."

"We got a time limit?" Reece returned, bristling at the order even knowing he shouldn't. This was what he came for—not making Lianna feel safe or to be a friend to Henry, but to get information.

"I'm giving you one. You give me something to go on by Monday night or I yank you and send Sabrina."

"Sabrina has all the subtlety of a horse."

"Your subtlety is costing us time and money. Maybe a heavier hand will do the trick."

Reece ran his free hand over his face. "Fine. Monday," he muttered, and ended the call before Shay could say anything else.

He looked through the woods. He couldn't see the

house this far in the trees, but he could see it in his mind's eye. Easily. Not just from a tactical stand-point but from a...a...

He *liked* the inn. Liked being here. Hell, he even liked taking pictures. Not so much the pictures them-selves, but the long walks and the paying attention to something other than what he had to do.

But he had things to do. And now he had a dead-line.

It was clear he was looking at this all wrong. Yeah, he felt guilty, but a conscience didn't keep Lianna and Henry safe. He had to get to the bottom of those listening devices, even if it violated her trust to do it.

He'd known her for only a few days. Guilt was misplaced. Where had this *softness* come from? Too much time between missions? Too little to go on for this assignment?

Too much time alone?

He shook away that thought and marched deeper into the woods. He couldn't go back to the inn until he had a hold of himself. Until he had a plan. He had to know if she had listening devices in her quarters by the end of the day Monday.

How would he do it? Lianna never seemed to leave the inn. The first step would be to find a time she did. She had to leave *sometimes*. He'd prefer it if Henry were gone, too. Anyway, Lianna wasn't likely to leave Henry behind.

He could probably convince Henry to let him into the personal quarters when Lianna was busy, but even *thinking* about using the kid that way made him feel ill. No, he couldn't use Henry. It wasn't right.

He went over plans, potentials, dismissing almost all of them as he trudged around the woods. The sun sank lower and lower, until it was nearly pitch-black. He didn't have a choice. He had to head back to the inn and figure…something out.

It was quiet when he made it back to the yard, but all the lights glowed warmly. Welcoming. It made him feel like he could belong here.

Which was the stupidest thought he'd possibly *ever* had. Even when he'd been a kid who'd thought a foster home could be permanent, that someone besides his parents could love him. At least he'd been a dumb kid then.

Now he was a grown adult.

You have a mission, Montgomery. Stop dancing around it.

The stars shone brilliantly above—he'd always had that, even as a kid. Starshine and endless space—and the hope there was something beyond the hell he'd lived in when he was still with his parents.

Now he was independent, doing what he was meant to do and helping people. It was stupid to beat himself up over a little guilt. If Lianna was the good person she seemed to be, then he was protecting her. He was doing his job by going through her personal things.

He closed his eyes and accepted a few things right here and now—so he could move on and deal with what had to be done.

He liked this place. He liked Lianna and Henry. He wanted them to be okay.

However, for them to be okay and safe, he had to

accept that he didn't belong here. He had to do his duty and get out.

He opened his eyes, gave himself a nod as if it was the physical shake he needed and headed inside. It was nearing eight o'clock, which meant Henry was likely in his room.

Reece had missed dinner, and though he didn't find himself particularly hungry, he knew that fuel was necessary no matter how a man felt. He moved for the kitchen, aware that he'd likely find Lianna there doing the dishes.

He wasn't disappointed. She hummed some nameless tune to herself as she rinsed off a dish and put it in the dishwasher.

She was beautiful. It was time to stop dancing around the truth. He liked her and was attracted to her, and that was what was holding him up. Now that he'd admitted it, if only to himself, he could move past it.

He retraced his steps, went all the way back to the front door, then made sure he made noise as he closed the door and walked heavier than necessary through the common areas, dining room and to the kitchen.

She looked over her shoulder as he came to a stop at the entrance to the kitchen. "There you are," she offered.

"Sorry I missed dinner. Stellar sunset."

She returned to loading the dishwasher. "You're a guest, Reece. No need to apologize. There's a plate of leftovers in the fridge. If you can wait about ten, I can serve you in the dining room. Or—"

"I could grab it myself. I don't want to get in your way. I *was* the one who missed the dining room hours."

"Well. I suppose that would be okay. Let me heat them up for you—" She made a move for the fridge, but he shook his head and made it there first.

"No need."

She held her wet, soapy hands in front of her, looking wholly perplexed. "But it won't be any good cold."

He smiled and took the plate from the fridge. "It's a very rare occasion I get a home-cooked meal. Hot or cold, it's still a treat."

She frowned at him, then let out a gusty sigh. "Well, if you're going to do that, you might as well eat at the kitchen table and not dirty up my dining room." She gestured to the small table he knew she and Henry often ate at, rather than joining guests in the dining room.

She gave Henry a life separate from the inn. Clearly on purpose. He wondered if it was to protect Henry, or for some other reason. One more in line with why he was here.

"You do an awful lot on your own," he said casually, settling himself at the table. "Don't most places have a cook and a maid and a handyman?"

She waved that away and went back to the dishes. "I have an on-call handyman, a maid service that comes in once a month to do a deep clean. But I usually don't have more than four or five guests. It isn't all that different than keeping house. Except I actually make some money off it."

"Do you ever leave?"

She huffed out a laugh. He wouldn't say she seemed *comfortable*, but she'd put her genial inn-keeper persona back in place. "Do parent-teacher conferences count? Sometimes I don't have guests, and those are usually the days for personal shopping or haircuts and taking Henry to the park. But I love this place. I like being close to home. Free days and errands are more than enough for me." She pushed a few buttons and then closed the dishwasher.

"So, if I wasn't here on Monday, and Henry was at school, you'd go into town and do errands?"

"Oh, maybe. Depends." She turned to face him. He watched her school her relief into something more casual. "Are you checking out?"

She wanted him to go, and that should not…hurt. "No. Not permanently, anyway. The park I want to go to is a bit of a drive. I thought I'd stay over, then drive back Tuesday. It might give you a chance to do that background check."

"Don't you have…? It's none of my business, of course, and I'm not trying to push you out. You've got our most expensive room, so your staying is good for my bottom line." She smiled. "Don't you have a home to get back to?"

"I like it here. It's…" He had to think and speak like a photographer, not like a man who'd never had a home. He looked at the plate in front of him. Pot roast, mashed potatoes and cooked carrots. It was delicious regardless of temperature. It was a dream.

He could hardly tell her he was having stupid home fantasies. "It's inspiring. I travel for my work.

Sometimes I find a place I like and stay awhile. If it's resulting in photos, that's all that really matters."

She nodded.

"If you ever don't want me here, you only have to say it."

"And have you leave me a bad review?"

"I wouldn't. I understand. You have to look out for yourself and your son. I've never…" He shook his head. This wasn't the way to assuage his guilt over needing to rifle through her things. He should be keeping his distance and getting the job done.

But she studied him, and there was something in her blue eyes that… It felt a bit like this place. Somewhere to be. Home.

Which convinced him he'd lost his mind. His objectivity. *Something.* He needed to get back to what he knew. Completing assignments and missions.

"You've never what?" she pressed.

"You're a good mother. You care about your son and want to protect him. I haven't really seen that." He shoved a bite of pot roast into his mouth and hoped to God it'd remind him to stop talking.

Her eyebrows drew together. "Your parents…"

He gave a shrug, trying to play it all off as casual. Unimportant. "Didn't care much about me. Enough neglect that the state took me away. I bounced around in fosters till I aged out."

"I'm sorry."

He shook his head, uncomfortable. But she was talking to him, studying him. Maybe she'd share some of her own past. Something about her dead husband. It was for the mission. A give-and-get.

Not his own soul.

"My parents couldn't take care of me, either, but my grandparents took me. I... They were great. But it's hard having parents who weren't. It always made me want to be better. And then Todd..." She sucked in a breath and then made a sound he thought was supposed to be a laugh. "Well, I have to go get Henry away from the screens and ready for bed. I allow him thirty minutes of playtime before he has to go to sleep."

She started walking out of the kitchen, and he should let her. Let her get back to her normal life, knowing on Monday he'd find the answer he was looking for, and hopefully be able to wrap this up in just a few more days.

But words came out anyway.

"If he still wants that story, I'd be happy to tell it. Wherever you're comfortable."

Chapter Four

Lianna stopped midstride. Not only had Reece remembered, but he was also casually offering to tell her baby a story. Something she knew Henry desperately wanted.

It was more care than the boy's own father had ever shown him. Which was saying next to nothing, but it still made Lianna's heart hurt. It made her... soft, when she had to stay strong for Henry.

Reece might like it here, he might be *inspired*, but he would leave. And Henry would be heartbroken to lose a companion, wouldn't he?

Or is that just what you tell yourself to keep you both safe?

She looked at Reece. He continued to eat, as if his offer was casual and any response she gave would be fine enough, but she saw something underneath that. Especially now that he'd mentioned his parents and foster homes. The military.

The man had no home. No family. He was lonely, and didn't she know that feeling? Intimately at that. This place had always been a balm to that loneliness, even when her grandparents weren't here. Why should she be surprised it reached out to someone else? It was what she counted on—people to view her inn as a charming home away from home.

Maybe he made her a little nervous, and caused those anxious thoughts to spiral, but the only way to deal with those reactions was to confront them. To *deal.*

"I'm sure he'd like that."

Reece gave a nod.

Lianna walked out of the kitchen but stopped just outside the door. Why would she get Henry ready for bed, then have him come back out to the common area? It made more sense to just have Reece come to Henry's room. What harm could a ten-minute story do?

Don't do it. You don't know him. The background check could come back and he could be a murderer. A rapist. He could be a con artist who wheedled his way into people's rooms and lives and...

She shook away the destructive thoughts. She wouldn't let Todd take her trust away from her. She wouldn't think the worst of everyone she came into contact with. Reece had been nothing but kind and good with Henry. He was just a lonely man.

And if he's some serial killer?

No. Not everyone was Todd. Echo and the Bluebird were supposed to be real life. She didn't want her real life to be full of silly suspicion and over-the-top fear.

"Why don't you come on back to his room?" Lianna heard herself say, or screech. She wouldn't leave him alone with Henry. She had a gun and pep-

per spray. She had a camera system and locks and...
She would not be paranoid. She was prepared.

When she turned to look back into the kitchen,
Reece had an arrested look on his face, fork half
way to his mouth.

He set the fork down at length. "You sure?"

Lianna kept her clenched fists behind her back
where he couldn't see them. "Of course. Just for tonight. He wants to show you his room. He needs a
bath first, and you need to finish your dinner. I'll
come get you in fifteen. There's ice cream in the
freezer."

With that, she turned on a heel.

And fled.

She was breathing heavily, heart beating in over-
time as she reached the door to her private quarters.
She had a special lock installed, a security camera
fastened to the ceiling that watched the door to see
who came and went.

She took precautions to keep herself and her child
safe.

*And now you've invited a stranger into your safe
space.*

She did some of the breathing exercises Dr. Winston had taught her. Calmed her ragged breathing.
They would still be safe. If she couldn't do this, if
she couldn't run her inn and have the occasional
connection to a guest, then they might as well move
back to Denver.

She eased into Henry's room, where he lay, head
hanging upside down off his bed, playing with his
handheld video game.

"I play even better upside down, Mom."

"Uh-huh. Time's up."

"Let me finish my level."

"Henry, we've talked about—"

"I can't save until I finish!" he yelled, as he did every night, furiously punching the keys as he raced her inevitable countdown.

"If you want Reece to come tell you his story in your room, the games better be off in five, four, three—"

Henry tossed the device onto his pillow and popped up on his knees. "You're going to let him come see my map?"

Lianna nodded, ignoring the way her chest clutched in fear.

"Really? Really!" Henry did a little dance.

Lianna blew out a breath. It was the right thing to do. Such a small thing, and it made Henry happy.

Once Reece told his story and left, she would be convinced she was fine, and they could live here forever.

And she'd never let this happen again.

She started Henry's bath and then left him to it, folding laundry just outside the bathroom so that she could listen for excessive splashing or anything out of the ordinary.

He chattered about Reece, about the map wall and the military and how jealous Joey would be that he'd be hearing *real* war stories.

Lianna cringed at that, but once she had Henry in his pajamas and ushered him into his room, she told him she'd return with Reece in a few minutes.

A kindness. For Henry. For a lonely man. Being kind to strangers was supposed to be a rewarding experience.

Lord, she was terrified. But Dr. Winston had told her she'd fall into this spiral. He'd warned her against taking on so much responsibility alone. He'd told her she wasn't ready.

Her hands clenched into fists as she walked back to the kitchen. He'd been wrong. She'd felt it deep in her bones. No matter how scarred she'd been by Todd's lies and death, she'd been determined to face the challenges head-on. At first for Henry, but then for herself, too.

She stepped into the kitchen, where Reece stood at her sink, drying off the dishes he'd used. He'd washed them, by hand.

It was kind of him to take care of it himself, but it was her job. *Her* job to attend to. Because she was the innkeeper and he was the guest and things were getting muddied.

But this weekend they'd have more guests and everything would…right itself.

For tonight she would prove to herself she could do a kindness for a stranger and not be punished for it. She forced a smile.

"Henry's all ready. And possibly too excited to sleep after."

"Military stories aren't that exciting," Reece said, carefully placing the cleaned dishes on the dish towel on the counter.

"Good," she said emphatically.

He turned, a rare smile flirting with the corners

of his mouth. He smiled at Henry a lot, but there was a gravity about Reece in general. A seriousness.

"I'm not sure where to put—"

She waved the dishes away. "Leave them there. I'll take care of it. You *are* the guest." She motioned for him to follow her.

She took him back through the hallway, then to the left, where her personal wing was blocked off from the rest of the house by a door. She pulled her key out of her pocket, watching out of the corner of her eye as Reece glanced at the security camera, at the lock. But he didn't comment on the precautions. He simply waited patiently.

So she let him into her private rooms and prayed to God she hadn't just made the biggest mistake of her life.

LIANNA DIDN'T WASTE TIME. She immediately walked down the narrow hall to the door farthest from the one they'd walked through. She opened the door and motioned Reece inside.

He stepped into a small room that screamed *little boy*. Action figures and video game posters, sports knickknacks and the faint smell of *sweat* under the lemon scent that permeated most of the inn. There was a baby monitor receiver on the windowsill— Reece knew Lianna clipped the main device to her belt when she did her early-morning or evening chores so she could hear Henry was safe and sound as he slept in his room. Just like she had the camera outside their private area. Lianna did everything she could to protect her son.

But as he'd mentioned to Shay, these were low-tech options a woman chose to make sure no guests took advantage of her and her son. Not someone trying to do any spying of her own.

Reece glanced up at the ceiling, and in less than five seconds, he saw it. This listening device was in the same place as it had been in his and the other guest rooms. A small unnoticeable sticker on the side of the smoke or carbon monoxide detectors in each room.

That was not from Lianna, and she definitely didn't know they were there. Someone was listening to her every move.

He didn't know how to react to that in the moment, so he could only look at Henry, who bounced on his bed in video game–themed pajamas, his blond hair a haphazard, damp mess.

Something inside of Reece's chest clutched. "Ready for a story?" he asked, his voice rusty as he lowered himself onto the too-small desk chair.

Lianna settled herself on Henry's bed, leaning against the wall, while Henry wiggled in the middle of the mattress.

He looked at the two of them. Henry a ball of energy, Lianna… He might have called her calm or serene if he couldn't sense all the tension tightening underneath the surface.

His presence in the room made her nervous, but she was powering through. So he'd tell his story quickly, make it just interesting enough to entertain Henry, and then…

He had no idea how he was going to tell her she

was being listened to. That she was still in danger. That he'd been lying to her about who he was. Because he was going to have to—whether Shay gave him the okay or not.

"I was stationed here for a while," he said, pointing to Afghanistan on Henry's map wall. "We were trying to…" Reece trailed off. He'd figured he'd throw out some story of something that had happened, not realizing how complicated it was when faced with the excited blue eyes.

"Protect people," Lianna supplied for him. "That's the job of the military, right?"

"Right. Right. Protect people." He wished it had been that simple. So distinctly black-and-white. He liked to think what he did now for North Star was clearer in terms of right and wrong, but the "bad guys" in any situation almost always thought they were the good ones.

"Did you drive a tank?" Henry asked.

"Not so much. It was more foot patrol. Walking around. Talking to people. Finding out who did what wrong and trying to…stop bad things from happening."

"Did you shoot people?" Henry asked earnestly, the wriggling slowing. The excitement dimming into something more like captivation. Not just about hurting the bad guys, but about what Reece himself had done.

"There were times we shot back at people shooting at us." There were no doubt things he'd done to end people's lives. But how did he explain that to a seven-year-old?

Luckily, Henry just kept right on asking questions. "Was it scary?"

"Very."

"What did you do when you were scared?"

"I depended on my training, but mostly my team. My fellow soldiers. I knew they had my back and I had theirs. You're all in it together."

"Like a family," Henry said softly.

Reece couldn't respond right away. His throat got too tight and the pain in his chest was almost unbearable. He stared hard at his shoes.

He had no family, but the army and then North Star had been as close as he'd ever gotten to almost feeling like he had one. "Yeah, I suppose."

In the end, he told no stories at all, just answered Henry's endless questions until the boy's eyes began to droop and Lianna insisted it was bedtime.

"Good night, Henry."

"Night, Reece. Thanks for the story." The boy yawned, long and loud. "You're the best."

Reece didn't have anything to say to that, though it was easy to tell Lianna wasn't pleased as she pulled back the covers and instructed Henry to crawl under them. She whispered a few words to Henry as Reece moved for the door.

He knew he should walk out of the room. Go up to his room to get his stuff and then right out the front door—away forever. Let Shay and the group hiring them handle the rest of this.

But instead he watched as Lianna smoothed the hair off Henry's forehead, gave him a kiss goodnight, whispered, *"I love you."*

You're all in it together.

Like a family.

Lianna met his gaze, something like sympathy in her eyes, as if she could see every untimely, unnecessary emotion on his face.

He turned abruptly and moved into the hallway. He looked back toward the door he'd entered. No doubt Lianna's bedroom was the door closest to that one. No doubt she kept herself as some kind of barrier to shield Henry from the outside world.

He'd never had anyone in his life shield him from anything. He'd learned to get over that—or thought he had. Army. North Star. He'd depended on himself and that had been good and right.

Lianna stepped into the hallway and closed Henry's door behind her. She looked at him enigmatically. "It was very kind of you," she said quietly. She had her innkeeper voice on. Courteous but firm. "But I don't think we'll be having a repeat performance."

Reece nodded stiffly. No. No repeat performances. No more letting himself get walloped by a ship that had sailed a long time ago.

He belonged to no one and no one belonged to him, and that was the way of his world. Nothing could change it. Wishing he could was useless. Pointless.

He reminded himself to move, to walk toward the door out. He glanced once more at her room door. He could barge in and show her exactly what he knew. But the listening device would hear.

And you don't want to hurt her.

She followed him to the door back to the main areas of the inn. He knew she still had chores to do out there, but she'd wait until Henry was asleep.

He had to tell her she was in danger. Surely someone listening to her every move meant she was in danger.

Or she's perfectly safe, because she knows nothing, and people have likely been listening for months without acting on it.

Regardless, he couldn't tell her here. He'd have to tell her outside. A note would be too long and complicated. This had to be done face-to-face and away from the bugs. Maybe he could catch her while she was gardening or walking to get Henry at the bus stop. He'd tell her and...

And what?

He knew she was waiting to close the door behind him. To lock him out. Where he belonged.

He knew he should *go*, but words tumbled out instead.

"For what it's worth... I know I shouldn't be attached, or care. I'm nobody. But I am and I do. So I'll keep my distance." He stepped out, headed for his room, without even a glance behind him.

He'd pack up and leave. Let Shay send in Sabrina to get the rest of the information. He'd gotten the first step figured out—Lianna didn't know she was being listened to.

Sabrina could do the rest. This was one assignment that was too... It was beyond him. He wasn't right for it. They could send him into danger, into the wilderness. Something remote and challenging. Not a widow and her cute kid.

This was too much. He couldn't do it. He just couldn't.

Chapter Five

Lianna went through her usual routine feeling like spun glass. As though one thing might shatter her into a million pieces.

She waited until she heard Henry's snores on the monitor. Would he ever be old enough for her not to need to hear his heavy breathing to know he was okay? It was just the house was so big, and she had so much to do.

She had to know he was safe. If that was paranoia, so be it. She'd let a stranger into their private quarters today. A stranger.

She leaned against the back door she'd been locking, squeezing her eyes against the lance of pain. Reece had sat there and answered Henry's questions with a patience and…a thoughtfulness Henry's own father had never given him.

He'd looked so wrong. His big frame taking up that small desk chair meant for a little boy. But the way he'd seemed so *arrested* and then devastated when Henry had said, *Like a family…* Lianna had wanted to be able to give Reece something. Anything to ease that heartbreaking look.

So you told him he couldn't do it again.

Yes, she'd had to.

Reece and his loneliness and lack of family were *not* her problems. Who knew? It could be all fabricated. Made up to make her sympathetic so he could do any number of terrible things.

She was being smart and safe. It wasn't anxiety, paranoia or fear. It was just common sense.

She walked through her evening responsibilities—making sure everything was in its place. She ended in the kitchen and stared at the dishes Reece had used and washed.

She didn't like this conflict inside of her. This inability to stick to a course of action. It reminded her too much of what she'd been in those last years with Todd. Someone who knew what she had to do, but had been too afraid to do it. Not because of any real threat, but because it required courage.

Lianna marched into the kitchen, put Reece's dishes and the clean ones from the dishwasher away. She would check to make sure the doors were locked, go to sleep and wake up with a clear head.

There'd be other guests here this weekend. Maybe that would help her work through all her conflicting feelings about Reece.

And maybe you should know better than to indulge in conflicting feelings about another man.

She stopped at the back door. It was locked, but instead of moving on to the front door, she turned the dead bolt. She stepped outside onto the much smaller back porch. She took a deep breath of the night air. The spring peepers were chirping and night rustled around her. Summer was trying to push through, but it hadn't arrived this far north yet. The moon and stars shone and everything was...

She'd felt so settled, and then Reece Conrad had walked into her inn and sent her into some kind of spiral.

It wasn't his fault. Whether he was a good man or an evil one, she was the only one who could control her life. Blaming paranoia on Todd didn't get her anywhere. Todd was dead. She was alive, and she had Henry.

It had been a rough year, with a lot of change, but Henry was thriving.

And what about you?

She wasn't there yet, no, but she could get there. She just had to work through what she was feeling. Not be afraid of it. Not hide it away.

So, here in the dark, she let herself cry. Racking sobs. She'd never let herself cry when she was married to Todd. Never let herself feel. She'd blocked it off and away deep inside to get through the day.

She had to keep a certain kind of control on the worst of her negative emotions around Henry, so as not to scare him, but that didn't mean she couldn't indulge when she was alone.

"Lianna."

She whirled around at Reece's voice, her heart beating too hard in her chest. And it wasn't just fear. It was something else. Something she hadn't allowed herself to feel in a long time.

"What is it? What's wrong?" he asked. It was dark, but in the moonlight it looked like he was scanning the woods around them. That was when she noticed he hadn't come out the back door; he was standing at the bottom of the porch stairs. Why would he have come around the front? Why…was he here? Asking her what was wrong when she was trying to have a good private cry?

She immediately wiped at her cheeks, hoping to… avoid *this*, whatever it was. "I thought you'd gone to bed."

"What's wrong?" he asked again, undeterred by her attempt at deflection.

"Nothing," she said, a little too shrilly. Or like a guilty child. "I just needed a moment to myself. The moon is pretty tonight. Excuse me, I have to—"

But he stepped in front of the door, stopping her from darting inside. Alarm spread through her and she tried to think of how she would fight this man who was so much bigger than her and… And carrying a bag.

"What are you doing?" she asked, sidetracked by the fact that he was carrying not just his camera bag in the middle of the night—which would have been strange enough—but the big duffel he'd shown up with, too.

He cleared his throat. "I heard you crying. I wanted to make sure you're okay."

"Are you leaving?"

"I…" He blew out a breath, and though he'd stopped her progress back inside, he kept his distance. A very careful distance. "I thought it would be best."

"Why?" And why was she asking why? He should

go. Disappear. Then she could go back to feeling settled.

But where would he go? How alone would he be? It made her heart pinch to think of him just going off with nowhere to go and no one to go home to.

He is not your responsibility.

"I thought you'd be more comfortable if I left."

She would be. It would be good, and yet… The thought of him leaving didn't settle her at all. "And quite a bit poorer."

"I'll pay for the full week."

How did he make her feel guilty? She had every right not to want a strange man to forge some bond with her child. To make her heart flutter and remind her of all the things she couldn't trust ever again.

But she felt a sinking sensation in her stomach and she couldn't… She couldn't just let him disappear into the night. "I think you misunderstand me. It's not that I don't… I have to worry. I'm a single woman in an isolated bed-and-breakfast. I have to worry. I have to be careful, but I was upset… It's hard. Watching Henry… He should have that kind of thing. A man to look up to, to answer his questions."

"He has you."

"Yes. I try to make it enough, but… When you're a mother, you want to give your child everything. I couldn't give him a decent father. I couldn't—"

"It's not your fault your husband was killed."

"Todd was no father before he was killed," Lianna said, the words as heavy as her heart. "I should have known… I should have gotten out. I should have done so many things. And it's not me dealing with the consequences—it's my child. I promised myself that wouldn't happen. Henry wouldn't pay for my mistakes with Todd. I failed there, and I can only hope to God he never knows what his father really was."

"What was he?"

"A very bad man." She shook her head. This wasn't Reece's problem. "I'd hate for you to sneak out on my account. I can't promise open doors or a lack of suspicion, but if I think you need to leave, I'll tell you."

Something crossed his face. Pain or guilt or something she was making up entirely. And he didn't agree with her or disagree. He didn't go inside. He only looked at her, something heartbreaking in his gaze.

"Lianna, do you know what a bug looks like?"

WHEN LIANNA ONLY looked at him in confusion, he knew she didn't have a clue.

"What kind of bug?" she asked, eyebrows drawn together, frown wrinkling her brow. "We have lots of them. I…"

Reece stood on her porch in the quiet, peaceful evening and knew he was about to ruin everything for her. He hated himself for it, but there were no other choices. Not now. "A listening device. Would you know how to identify a listening device?"

She stiffened. Immediately. Any confusion in her gaze turned cold. He could tell from the way her eyes widened and darted toward the house—as if his mentioning them would make them suddenly visible to her—that she didn't know about them. And his mentioning any kind of listening device made her immediately afraid. Of him.

Good. It was time she understood who she was dealing with. No more guilt. Just the cold, hard truth.

She edged away from him, but then seemed to realize her son was inside the building he was blocking her from. Her hands curled into fists, as if she was ready to fight him tooth and nail.

He'd win. Easily. But he didn't want to fight her.

He moved to the side, so that if she wanted to dart for the door, she could. But he spoke as he did it. "There is a listening device fastened to the smoke or carbon monoxide detector in each of the rooms in your house. I haven't checked your room, but I can only assume you have one, as well."

"What are you even talking about?" she said, her voice strangled.

"I saw the one in my room first. Then I searched the rest of the inn. Someone wants to know what you know, Lianna."

"How do I know *you* didn't put them there?" she demanded.

"I guess you don't. But I haven't been in your room. I'm sure your camera could prove that."

She inched closer and closer to the door. "What are you…? *Who* are you?"

He blew out a breath. How to answer that? If he was smart, he'd lie. A man who'd done what he'd done for as long as he'd done it knew better than to be *honest*.

"You know what? Don't bother answering, since it

will clearly be a lie. Go. And don't ever come back. If this is about Todd… I don't know anything about him. I never did. I just want you to leave me alone. All of you."

"What do you mean *all*?"

"All the men who bothered me in San Francisco, and then again in Denver. I told the FBI and whoever else everything I knew. If they thought I was going to change my mind because…because…"

The FBI. That was something North Star could check into. Reece didn't get the impression they were the ones asking North Star for help, but Todd Kade could have had ties to the FBI or an FBI case under his real name.

"You were going. Please don't let me stop you," she said, now standing in the door. He could see she had a death grip on the knob. She'd slam the door in his face, try to fight him off with everything she had.

He'd made a mess of things. And there was no one to blame that on but himself. He'd gone soft, or lost an edge somewhere along the way. He'd failed… everything.

So, yes, he should go. Drive back to North Star. Give his report on everything he knew. If they needed more from Lianna, they could send Sabrina. Leave him out of it.

And what? Prove to Lianna she can't trust anyone even with her husband dead?

Lianna couldn't be his problem, but Shay wasn't going to keep him around if he failed this very simple mission. There was no reason for her to, and North Star was everything.

Reece scrubbed a hand over his face. "We only wanted to help."

"We?" she all but screeched. "Who is we?"

Before he could explain that he *couldn't* explain, she held up a hand.

"No. I don't want to hear another lie. Just…go." And with that, she stepped fully inside and closed the door. The lock clicked into place, and no doubt she'd set the alarms, as well.

Reece stood there in the dark. He knew she was watching, waiting to make sure he left. Then she'd likely go check on Henry. She wouldn't sleep tonight. She'd be too worried.

He blew out a breath. She'd been crying over everything she couldn't give Henry because he'd had a father who didn't care. But Lianna didn't seem to understand that having a mother who cared like she did would give any kid the chance at a really good life.

Unless whoever put those listening devices comes for them.

Reece had to get to the bottom of it. He couldn't just leave her to the wolves. He'd messed it all up, but he could hardly leave that mess and not clean it up. Not when she and Henry could be in potential danger.

Sabrina wasn't the answer. He hadn't been able to lie to Lianna and Henry any longer. His failing, sure, but that didn't mean the whole mission had to be a failure.

He glanced at his watch. Late, but not too late, hopefully. As he walked toward his car, bags still strapped to his back, he slid his phone out of his pocket.

"Hello," a woman's voice grumbled into the receiver.

"Elsie? I need your computer expertise."

"Reece, do you know what time it is?" Elsie Rogers said over a yawn. She was a newer member of North Star, but her computer skills were unparalleled. She also didn't go into the field, which meant Reece could tell a few half-truths to keep her from reporting everything to Shay.

"Sorry, this can't wait. I need you to hack into the computer and security systems here, and I figure that will take a while."

"That bed-and-breakfast where you're staying? They're not even on a server. I'll have it cracked in fifteen minutes."

"Great. I'll call you back in fifteen." He hung up before she could protest or ask for more information. He threw his bags into his car and turned on the ignition. He could see the shadow of Lianna in the attic window—she'd likely gone up there to make sure he hadn't left anything sinister behind.

Nothing sinister. Just a note for her, and one for Henry.

She stood there in the window, clearly watching and waiting to make sure he left. He wasn't going anywhere.

But Lianna didn't need to know that.

Chapter Six

So Reece Conrad was a liar in a long line of liars. Li-anna shouldn't be surprised and she really shouldn't be hurt. He was a stranger. If the man she'd been married to for six years could lie to her, day after day, year after year, why wouldn't some stranger posing as a guest at her inn be able to?

She frowned. Sheriff Reynolds had said Reece's background was clear, and that it existed. Surely he hadn't given her his real name. Was he as deceitful as Todd? Going around taking on other identities. Or had he stolen someone's identity? Or…

It didn't matter. It did *not* matter. He was a liar—no matter how he did it.

She looked at the letters he'd left on the desk in his room. She wouldn't read them. She certainly wouldn't give one to Henry. They'd known each other a few days. It was hardly worth…letters.

Once he'd pulled away in his car, she'd left his room, armful of bedding and those letters in hand. She dumped the bedding in the laundry room, checked the locks three times, checked on Henry even though the sound that came through the baby monitor hooked

to her belt was still nothing more than the soft snuf-
fling of his snores.

She stood in the doorway of his dark room, watching the lump of blankets that was her son. Her safe,
sleeping son. Reece had been here in his room. Lianna had let that happen, and Reece had talked to
Henry and answered his questions and looked as
though…

Well, if he was a smarter bad guy he would have
used Henry to get information out of her. So he was
either very stupid or…

*He is the bad guy. He is. Don't you dare be this
foolish over a man ever again.*

She turned away from Henry and forced herself
to go to her bedroom. The locks were locked. The
security measures were in place. And it turned out
she should definitely listen to her gut, because it had
told her Reece was bad news.

Well, no. Her gut had told her the opposite. Her
brain had told her Reece was bad news. So from here
on out, she'd listen to her brain and her paranoia, because clearly they were right.

Except Reece left of his own accord. Some bad guy.

So maybe he wasn't all bad. Maybe, unlike Todd,
he had some kind of conscience. He still wasn't who
he'd said he was. He was still a *liar* who knew about
listening devices and had been sneaking around her
inn, either finding them or placing them.

Lianna flipped on the light in her room. There'd be
no sleeping tonight. Should she even bother trying?

She glanced up at the smoke detector above her
doorway. It was the same innocuous device she had

in every room. The little green light was on as it always was, showing that the batteries were still good. She had a note in her ledgers of when to change the batteries so guests were never woken up by that annoying beeping reminder.

Still, she stared at it. She didn't see anything out of the ordinary. Anything attached. Certainly nothing Reece would have been able to see just by looking.

She marched over to her desk, dropped the letters she would definitely throw away and pulled her chair over to place it under the smoke detector. Maybe he was lying about the listening devices, too. Maybe this was some kind of mind game.

She found herself thinking Reece would never do that, but she had to remember she didn't really know him. That wasn't even his real name. Who even knew *what* he was.

He probably worked for the same people Todd had. Or was with the FBI. Maybe some elite military group. Maybe all three. God knew Todd liked to spread his "talents" around.

Whatever it was, it had *nothing* to do with her. She only wished the ghost of Todd Kade would stop haunting her.

She got up on the chair. She inspected the smoke detector. She didn't really see anything. Well, a little piece of plastic that looked like a stray piece of tape, maybe? Of course, she wouldn't have put any tape on her smoke detector.

She reached up and touched it, then pulled the edge. There was *something*. She pulled it harder.

Slowly a thin piece of adhesive came off, revealing a small circle that looked almost like a coin with holes in it.

She didn't fully understand how something so small and flimsy could be a listening device, but this was something she definitely hadn't put there, and it most certainly didn't belong on a smoke detector. Whatever it was, someone had been in her house and put something foreign on her smoke detector.

Reece could have put it there. Yes, she had cameras, and she always zipped through the videos when they had guests just to make sure nothing was amiss. She hadn't seen Reece.

But he could probably hack computers. He could probably...

She curled her fingers around the device. He'd told her the truth. In this, he'd told her the truth. Which could be a trick, but had Todd ever told her even a tiny bit of the truth? Even to mess with her?

She wouldn't go chase him down, of course. But maybe she should take his warning at face value. Maybe she should call Sheriff Reynolds tomorrow and have him take a look at the listening devices.

She looked at the one in her palm. She thought about saying something inflammatory. Like "Screw you and leave me alone." It would be satisfying.

And stupid.

She got down from the chair and placed the listening device on her desk. Was someone actively listening? Or were they just recording her? What would they be after?

No one could possibly know what she knew about

Todd. Not Henry, not the FBI, not her parents or grandparents or the stray acquaintance. No one knew what she'd seen in that file.

She thought about the way the FBI agent had brought her into his office in San Francisco. How nervous she'd been. They'd said, "Sorry for your loss," and she hadn't known what to say.

Todd being dead had been a relief, which had made her feel terrible at the time. No one should be relieved that their own husband and child's father was dead. But she had been.

Then...it had gotten so complicated she didn't even feel guilty about her relief anymore. Questions from the FBI, and a couple of other men in suits who'd claimed to be Todd's associates. The move to Denver, where they'd all followed her. With constant questions.

None of them had threatened her. If anything, they treated her like Todd had treated her. Like a stupid liability.

And if she was honest with herself, as it had gone on and on, she'd played up that role. Convincing them of her stupidity and ignorance. So much so that she'd been able to see Todd's real name in that file, and the name of two of the groups the FBI thought he was working with.

She'd never uttered Todd's real name, never so much as even googled the group names. She'd packed up Henry, moved home to Echo and convinced herself she could keep Henry safe by resolutely *not* knowing what she knew.

Lianna sank onto her bed. Who was listening to

her? The FBI? One of the other groups? Did it matter when she'd never given them any reason to believe she knew what she knew?

She blew out a breath and had to reconcile the fact that in comparison to everyone who had come before, Recce had never asked her anything. Not one question about what she knew or who Todd was. Oh, she'd offered up a few things, but nothing people wouldn't be able to find out.

Especially people who know how to recognize a listening device as small as that at a glance.

Maybe she'd been too hasty. Maybe Reece could have helped her.

She shook her head. That was stupid. No one could help her. Just like always, she had to help herself.

And she would. She'd do whatever she could to keep her and her son safe. Destroy those letters, forget Reece Conrad had ever existed, and…and…

She would figure it out. She had to.

REECE HAD BEEN conditioned from birth to survive on little sleep. His parents hadn't kept normal hours, and had never allowed him a full night, from what he could remember. There hadn't been a foster home he'd been able to relax in enough to fully sleep. Then he'd put those habits and skills to good use in the military and his work with North Star.

Including right now. He'd camped the past three nights in the woods a good two miles from the Bluebird. He kept watch, harassed Elsie about what she could find through Lianna's computer files, and he did not mention to Shay or anyone else that he'd had a little blip of conscience and was no longer precisely *at* the Bluebird.

He slept in short patches of time in order to keep his mind sharp and his response times quick, but mostly it was like being on patrol in Afghanistan again. Watching. Waiting. Without fully knowing what for.

He dialed Elsie, knowing she wouldn't appreciate the early-morning call. Still, he couldn't help himself.

"I told you I'd call if I found anything," she said by way of greeting. She sounded grumpy and aggrieved. He didn't blame her one bit, but that didn't mean he was going to back off.

"I just wanted to check in."

"Whoever put in those listening devices did it a long time ago, and my guess is they knew enough about computers to bypass the inn's remedial security measures." She paused and audibly yawned. "I don't think we're going to catch the guys on tape. I've been through it until my eyes are dead, and no one aside from the woman and the boy go into her or his room."

"How remedial are the security measures?" Reece demanded. He was close and he'd been watching, but…that sounded worse than he'd assumed.

"It'd keep a common criminal out, but I don't think we're dealing with the common criminal."

No, they weren't. "What about files?"

"Reece, I only have two hands."

"And I've got all day."

"I've already told you it'd take all day to download anything on your hot spot. Unless you plan on getting closer to civilization and a better signal, you're out. I could walk you through hacking into her computer and you could go through that yourself, but again, bad internet means slow hacking."

It would have been tricky to find that kind of time even if he was still a guest at the Bluebird. But he was not, and he wasn't ready for North Star to know he'd messed up yet. And hopefully wasn't ever going to be honest about that part.

"So whoever planted the devices got around the cameras," he said.

"Or she deleted the older footage, though usually I can dig that up, too."

"She wouldn't have deleted it."

"Getting to know her, then?"

Reece didn't say anything to that. He needed more to go on. He needed *something*. "What about reservations? Can you look into those?"

"Of course, but to what end?"

"I doubt someone broke in when they could easily be a guest and plant things. Find someone with a fishy background."

"You want me to go back through almost a year's worth of reservations and look at everyone's background?"

"Why not?"

Elsie sighed. "Oh, no reason at all," she muttered.

"Start at the beginning." Reece thought of his conversation with Lianna on the porch. He hadn't seen any listening devices outside, and he'd definitely looked. Still, it didn't hurt to be cautious. "But check this weekend, too. Any new reservations this weekend I want to know about ASAP."

"Anything else, sir?" Elsie asked dryly.

"I promise to keep you drowning in those disgusting sour candies you love so much when this is all over."

She made a slight huffing noise. "You're starting to act like Holden, you know that?"

"Well, there's no need to be insulting."

She chuckled. "All right. I'll see what I can dig up. But I'm holding you to the candy."

"Got it. Thanks, Elsie." He hung up the phone and shoved it into his pocket, then went about cleaning up his camp.

Though he planned on sleeping here every night until...well, until there was no reason to, he didn't leave any trace of him behind on the off chance someone came out hiking this way during the day.

Once everything was packed into his backpack, he walked up to the road, where he kept out of sight but made sure Lianna got Henry safely on the bus. He watched the area to make sure no one else was paying too close attention to the woman and her child.

Then, as the bus rumbled away and Lianna walked back to the inn, he got in his car and drove the bus route, a plan he'd worked on all weekend. Everything went according to plan, including pulling into the subdivision next to the school where he could see through the backyards of houses and to the bus drop-off.

Once Henry was safely inside the school, Reece could convince himself all was well and return to be closer to the Bluebird.

He returned to his hiding spot near the Bluebird, parking his car in a wooded area he'd found that kept the car out of sight of any passerby. It was a good two miles direct from the Bluebird, and a five-mile drive since no roads went through the woods. Besides, as far as he knew, only Lianna was aware of the kind of car he was driving, and he'd never seen her drive anywhere. If she did, she'd be heading into town, he had to assume, and this was the opposite direction.

He was surprised when his phone went off and Elsie's number was on the screen. She'd found something. God, he hoped she'd found something, to be calling back so soon.

"Got something?" Reece demanded, getting out of the car.

"I started with this weekend's reservations," she said with no preamble. "One reservation Friday night. Made late at night, which is kind of weird, though not unheard of. Still, I looked into the guy. His background is fake."

"How do you know?"

"What do you mean, how do I know? I make up fake backgrounds for you guys myself. I know what to look for when it comes to fake records. He's fake."

"Who is he?"

"That I don't know, and won't be able to find out without a picture or a fingerprint or something more tangible. He's checking in this afternoon, according to the reservation. Get me something I can use, and I'll figure out who he is."

Reece rubbed his free hand over his jaw. Late at night. Someone had overheard his argument with Lianna. Which meant she was in danger.

And it was all his fault.

Chapter Seven

Lianna prepared the attic room for her new guest, erasing every last shred of evidence Reece—or whatever his name was—had ever been here.

Why should a man who'd spent less than a week at her inn leave such a…void? It didn't make any sense, and it made her hate him even more than she already did. She'd been safe and happy, for the most part, before he ruined everything with his listening devices and heartbroken eyes.

He probably had a family. A big one. He probably had three wives and twenty kids and great parents.

If she kept telling herself that, maybe she could erase the memory of his expression when Henry had said, *Like a family.*

The alarm on her phone went off, signaling it was time to walk up to the bus stop to pick up Henry. He'd been sullen all weekend, with Reece gone and two older women exclaiming over how cute he was.

The cruelest of all comments, in Henry's estimation. Still, he'd bounded off to school with his normal restless energy, eager to spend time with Joey and other kids his age. Even if reading was *stupid.*

She really needed to plan another playdate for Henry and Joey, but her schedule was so packed, and she hated feeling like she was making the Hendersons' lives difficult by always needing them to handle transportation.

It was weirdly nice to have the normal worries in her mind as she began her walk to the bus stop. She'd much rather worry about mom stuff than...danger.

Hopefully her new reservation wouldn't arrive early, but if he came in before she got Henry home, she'd be able to wave him down from the road. No one came down her road unless they were looking for the Bluebird.

As if on cue, she heard the pop and rumble of tires on gravel. A sleek black car with tinted windows appeared around the curve. It looked like a very... *official* car. But it was the make and model the man had given her on his reservation form.

She waved and the car slowed, coming to a stop next to her. The window rolled down and the driver leaned toward her. He wore big aviator sunglasses and he made no move to take them off, despite the gloomy weather.

"Hello," Lianna offered. "Are you Mr. Adams?"

The man smiled. "Yes, ma'am."

She had to ignore the jitter of nerves. Reece couldn't make her distrust every single man who came to her inn. She forced a smile in return. "I'm Lianna Kade and I run the Bluebird. I'm just picking up my son at the bus stop. You go on ahead and let yourself inside. I'll be there in just a moment to check you in.

There's coffee in the common area. Make yourself comfortable."

"Thanks."

She gave a little nod, then continued walking up to the main road. She looked back once at the car. It was just a car. He was just a guest. Just a man.

But she was beginning to wonder how she'd sleep at night every time a lone man came to stay at the inn. How was she going to ever let Henry out of her sight? How was life *ever* going to be normal?

"Thanks a lot, Reece Conrad, or whoever you are."

She reached the road and glanced at her watch. Just another minute or two and the bus should show up.

She took a deep breath. She'd be extra cautious when it came to having strange men stay at her inn, but that didn't mean she had to ban them entirely. She'd just protect herself. And keep Henry completely separate.

She didn't like the way he'd looked at her. It had been…cold. A very fake friendliness. Reece had—

Good God, Lianna, you cannot live in fear.

Sheriff Reynolds had always been kind enough to offer a deputy or even himself if she ever felt uncomfortable. She knew in part because he'd been good friends with her grandparents and they'd asked him to watch after her, but also because he was a nice man. Always had been.

She wouldn't be too proud to ask for help. In fact, maybe she'd offer a free room to the sheriff and his wife for tonight. Or Joey and his parents. Yes, she'd fill up the inn with friends. Make it a party.

And drag them into what Todd started and Reece brought up all over again?

No. She wouldn't think like that. She'd— She whirled around at a noise—a crack, a footstep, something.

And there he was.

Reece held up his hands as if she had a weapon trained on him. She certainly wished. But all she had were too ineffectual fists. "What are you doing here?"

He dropped his hands and stepped closer. When she jumped back, he paused his approach. "Lianna, I'm going to need you and Henry to come with me."

Go with him? She forced a caustic laugh out of her mouth even though she felt shaky with fear. What was he doing here? What was he playing at? "I'm not going anywhere with you."

"Your new guest isn't safe."

It sent a bolt of icy fear down her spine, but she refused to show it. "And you are?"

"I know you don't believe me, but yes. I am."

"I told you to go, Reece. If that's your name."

"It's my name."

"Sure."

"Lianna… The man who made this reservation… There's too much of a coincidence to the timing. I didn't find any listening devices outside, but maybe he overheard our conversation."

Lianna stilled. She had taken the listening device off the smoke alarm and shoved it into her desk drawer. Would whoever was listening know she'd tampered with it? Obviously. It would have changed what they could hear.

"Wait. How do you know about this man's reservation?"

Reece's expression didn't change, but she thought she saw a flash of something like guilt in his eyes as the bus rumbled around the corner.

"You and Henry. Come with me. It's for your own good. I promise."

"You're insane to think I'd do that. To think I'd leave my business. When you admitted to lying to me."

"Yes, admitted, and I'll gladly admit a lot more. But you have to come with me."

"Neither Henry nor I will be going *anywhere* with you, and if you keep pestering me, I will call the police."

"You can go back to the inn. Fine," Reece said, and impatience was snapping at the edges of his calm, controlled voice. "You're an adult and you have free will to put yourself in danger, but you can't put Henry in danger."

"*I* am Henry's mother."

"You're right. And, honestly, I'm not letting you go, either."

"Not letting me? What are you going to do? Force me?"

"If I have to."

"You are out of your mind." The bus door opened and Henry bolted out, already yelling Reece's name and rushing toward him.

"Reece, you're back!"

"I am. And you know what, Hank? We're going to play a game."

"We are?"

Lianna moved to step in between them. "No." She should be afraid, but she couldn't seem to access fear over the hot sputter of fury. "We are not going to—"

In a move she didn't anticipate, Reece was behind her and then effectively throwing her over his shoulder. It was all very smooth and sudden and even gentle.

So much so that she didn't even protest immediately. She could only blink at the grass bumping along underneath her head.

"That's funny," Henry was saying, and she could see his tennis shoes happily prancing next to Reece's steady strides. She didn't even bump against him as he walked with her over his shoulder.

His *shoulder*. She managed to break through the shock and confusion and twisted in his grasp.

"Put me down! This isn't funny. I'm going to…" She didn't know what. Kick him? Scream?

Henry was prancing beside them, laughing hysterically. They were being kidnapped, essentially, and her child was laughing.

And you're allowing it.

REECE KNEW IT wasn't a laughing matter, but Henry's sheer joy at Reece lugging around his mother had his own mouth curving into a smile.

"You're going to be in *so* much trouble when you

put her down." Henry giggled as Reece led them into the woods.

He didn't know how much time they had, but Sabrina would arrive shortly to take care of the man at the inn.

Ideally the man poked around a little bit first, giving Elsie a chance to fully ID him. Then Sabrina could swoop in and take care of him. If things didn't go ideally? Well, they'd roll with the punches.

Lianna twisted in his grip. He could feel her tense her body as if she was going to punch or kick, but she never did anything. Except demand he put her down as he carried her into the woods.

"What are we doing? Where are we going?" Henry asked.

"We're going to take a secret trip."

"We are not. We are absolutely not taking a trip. Henry…" She trailed off, and Reece realized she didn't know how to yell at him without scaring Henry, and Henry was her first priority.

He couldn't even imagine what it would have been like to have a mother or any foster parent who cared that much if he was afraid. How different his life would have been.

Didn't matter. His life was the way it was, and he'd made some mistakes here, but he would not allow Lianna and Henry to pay for them. Even if Lianna ended up hating him.

"I promise. Once we get to my car, Lianna, you'll have as many answers and reassurances as I can give you."

"Yes, that's known advice," she muttered into his

ear. "Go with the crazy man to a second location and let him explain everything to you."

He chuckled in spite of himself and all the danger he was in. *She* was in. Maybe Elsie couldn't prove the new reservation was after Lianna yet, but the timing was too suspect. Reece was sure that once Elsie ID'd him, they'd be able to pin him to the group that North Star's client was after.

Lianna didn't say anything else, and she didn't fight him. Oh, he could practically hear the wheels turning in her head. She was probably paying attention to the surroundings and planning her escape once he let her down.

Reece could hardly blame her.

He reached the car and gently put her down on her feet, knowing she'd grab Henry and try to bolt. Except, maybe she wouldn't, because that would scare Henry.

"I've got a computer in the car," he said, before she could grab Henry and run. "It has all my files. Who I am. Missions I've been on, both in the military and for the group I currently work for, including this one. The only thing that's been redacted is the name of my group and the people I work with—which is for your safety as much as theirs. You can listen to phone calls I made while I was staying here. They're all recorded. I know... I get it. You can't trust me. You shouldn't, but I want to help, and I want you to understand that... I'm here to help you."

"Why do we need help?" Henry asked, blinking up at Reece. His face clouded. "Is this about my father?"

As someone who was adequately familiar with that acidic feeling toward one's father, Reece still felt his heart pinch. He wanted to assure Henry he was safe, and Reece would make sure everything was taken care of, but...

Reece glanced at Lianna. He didn't want to step on any toes. He didn't want to hurt Henry *or* Lianna.

Lianna slid her arm around Henry. "Yes, sweetheart. But it's going to be okay."

"You're going to make it okay. Right, Reece?" Henry asked, smiling up at him, hope and something like adoration lighting up his features.

Reece wished he'd turn into primordial ooze right then and there. "I'm going to do everything I can. I just need you both to trust me, and you know, that's rough, because you shouldn't trust people you just meet. Trust should be earned, and I haven't earned it."

"That's okay," Henry said, with a seven-year-old shrug.

Reece looked at Lianna again, knowing it was very much not okay. "The computer is in the back of the car."

"Why would I get in the back of your car?"

Reece sighed and pulled the computer out of the back seat. He handed it to her, along with some headphones. "Sit wherever you like. Look at whatever you like."

"You could have made all this up. It could be fake," she said, not taking either device.

"You're absolutely right," he agreed. He stepped close enough he could lower his voice so Henry wouldn't hear. "But it's an awful lot of work to convince you I'm a good guy when I could just as easily throw you and Henry in that car and drive you where I want to take you."

Her scowl was so deep, her blue eyes practically a flame of rage, and yet she said nothing. He stepped back and waited for her response.

"What about the man who I'm supposed to be checking in?"

"We're getting a clear ID on him. Then, if he's who we think he is, we'll handle it."

"Who's we?"

"My associates. Once they handle it, your inn will be locked up while we try to figure out the rest. You don't have any reservations for the week, so that shouldn't eat into business. If we can't get you back by Saturday, we'll figure something out."

"How do you know my reservations?" she demanded.

Reece sighed. "Do you really want to know?"

"Yes, I…" Then she closed her eyes and shook her head. "No. No."

"So can we speed this along?"

She took the computer and the headphones with a jerk and stomped over to the hood of the car. She settled herself against it, put the headphones in her ears and kept her eagle gaze split between the screen and Henry.

Henry shed his backpack and chased a butterfly for a few seconds. Reece knew he should keep his mouth shut, but the kid entertaining himself… Yeah, he'd been there. Henry had Lianna, of course, but there was still likely to be some loneliness, given the somewhat isolated life he lived, without a father figure.

Reece swallowed at the rust in his throat and moved to the trunk. Lianna looked like she was about to charge him, as if she was afraid he was going to toss Henry in the trunk. He knew he deserved her suspicion, but that didn't make it easy.

He popped it quickly and grabbed a baseball glove and held it up before she could dive at Henry.

"Hey, Hank, you want to play catch?"

Henry perked up, looking at the glove in Reece's hand. "Here?"

"Your mom has some reading to do before we can go on our trip. Not much room with the trees, and I've only got one glove, but it might pass the time."

"Yeah, cool."

Reece tossed the glove at Henry, who caught it with a fumbling grab. "I played T-ball last year, and this year we're actually going to pitch."

"That's cool. You got a team?"

"Giants."

"Giants? You can't be serious."

Henry giggled. "They're awesome."

Reece scoffed. "West Coast teams," he said with mock indignation. "Don't have any heart." He tossed the ball at Henry, with an eye on Lianna. She was watching them, but not with that same suspicious gaze. It was something that made his lungs squeeze.

Henry tossed the ball back and Reece caught it bare-handed, fumbling with the catch when usually he was as sure-handed as they came.

"Who's your favorite team?"

"Huh?" Reece focused back on Henry and playing catch. He cleared his throat. "Twins all the way."

"The American League! DH is cheating!" Then Henry erupted into a fit of giggles, clearly a fight he enjoyed having with someone in his life. Not his father, maybe the grandfather or the great-grandfather.

Because the boy wasn't alone like Reece had been. He had love and a family, and Reece would do good to remember to keep his distance.

Somehow.

Chapter Eight

The first thing Lianna did was pull up the file marked REECE CONRAD MONTGOMERY. She was absolutely certain it was fake, since it mirrored everything he'd told her almost exactly.

Born in South Dakota, became a ward of the state at age ten, where he spent the next eight years jumping from group home to foster home and back again. Enlisted in the army at eighteen, served for twelve years, including two tours of Afghanistan. There were all sorts of cross-references to missions.

Everything looked…real. There were enlistment records and school records. There was even a birth certificate.

He was right. It was an awful lot of effort to convince her he was the good guy when he could have just…kidnapped them.

Though he *had* grabbed her. So. He wasn't… perfect. Even if it had been careful and gentle and…

She couldn't believe this was happening. She couldn't believe she was considering going with him. This had to be lies. It had to be.

She opened a folder labeled PHONE CALLS.

Each file was named with a date and time, and each date was one of the dates he'd spent at her inn.

The first one was his conversation with a woman. She seemed like a boss, or at the very least a co-worker. They talked about the listening devices and getting into her room.

Lianna almost turned it off. It felt like an invasion of privacy to listen to him like this, even though it was his idea. Even though he was discussing invading *her* privacy. It felt wrong to hear him *plan* to get into her room.

We want to keep the widow and the kid out of it, don't we? That's a priority for me. Kids don't get caught in the cross fire.

She didn't hear what came next. That echoed in her ears instead. He said it so...fervently. Like he really meant it.

She glanced up at him. He wasn't smiling anymore. That look from the other night was on his face as he caught the ball Henry lobbed at him.

Loneliness.

She shook her head. She couldn't be fooled again. But everything on this computer...well, it pointed to a good man whose job it was to help people.

He'd helped take down a murderer by posing as a gang member. He'd saved a young girl from being kidnapped into the same gang. He'd done all sorts of things to protect people from this Sons of the Badlands group. All while working for some mysterious, nameless group.

A group who'd been approached to find out more about Todd's death. And what she knew.

Lianna chewed on her lip. Reece obviously wanted what she knew. But he didn't know she knew much of anything. And he hadn't been pushy like all the men who'd come before. He hadn't demanded answers or made her feel stupid.

No, he played you.

Lianna blew out a breath, listened to another phone call where he reiterated keeping Henry out of it. He sounded frustrated and…

She didn't know because she didn't know *him*, and she was fooling herself if she thought she could just tell. Hadn't life taught her she was a terrible judge of character?

She opened another folder, labeled LETTERS, hoping to find some clarification. Some…sign to point her in the right direction. A flat-out lie. *Something* she could use to convince her she should walk away.

Instead, she found the letters Reece had left for her and Henry. Letters she'd shoved in her drawer with the listening device and hadn't read.

Oh, she'd come close a few times, but she'd known that if she read them, she might feel some misplaced sense of grief, and she had enough real grief in her life. But now…

She opened the first one and read the short letter.

Dear Lianna,
Thank you for letting me into your home. Not just the bed-and-breakfast, but your life and Henry's. I'm sorry I couldn't stay and enjoy

it longer. If you should ever need anything,
please don't hesitate to contact me.
Reece

It didn't say much. It didn't say anything, except
the offer to be in touch. To help. How did a lonely
man, clearly in desperate need of a family, get into
the business of helping strangers?

She opened Henry's letter, and it was more of
the same.

Hank,
Sorry I had to rush out without saying good-
bye. I had an emergency to take care of. If
you'd like to contact me, your mom has my
information. Hope to see you again someday.
Keep asking questions.
Reece

Neither said anything particularly groundbreak-
ing or poignant. So why did she feel like crying?
Like he was the only one she could trust, when it
could be an act.

It's some act.

She looked up at Henry and Reece. Reece made
an impressive one-handed grab that had Henry hoot-
ing with delight and Reece grinning.

Yes, he could be acting. She'd learned just how
good at acting people could be. But this was all so
unnecessary. So over-the-top. Unless he was who he
said he was. Unless he really wanted to help them.

If he was the bad guy in this scenario, there were

a million horrible ways he could have tried to get information out of her or Henry.

She couldn't discount the fact he might be a bad guy with some kind of conscience, but she'd been interrogated before. By men with less…everything. Even the FBI agents, who she had to believe were trying to do the right thing, had been cold and off-putting. Dismissive at times.

Reece was none of those things.

You're really going to trust the guy who carried you away from the bus stop like a sack of mulch? Leave your inn to whoever? Run away? Again?

A phone rang. Reece pulled his mobile out of his pants pocket. "Montgomery," he answered, tossing the ball to Henry and then holding up a hand to pause their game.

Henry busied himself by throwing the ball high in the air and then darting around in an attempt to catch it. Reece's expression was grim and serious as he gave terse responses to whoever was on the other end.

When he shoved the phone back in his pocket, his gaze met hers. It was direct, and something shivered through her that wasn't fear. It was something she couldn't possibly allow herself to name.

He walked over to her, digging something else out of his pocket.

"Our operative at the Bluebird needs backup." He handed her the keys to his car. "If you want to drive away, that's fine. Just go. Don't come back until someone gets in touch with you with the all clear."

Lianna blinked. "Wh-what?"

But Reece had dropped the keys and was already backing into the trees. "If you want to stay, I'll be back soon."

"But—" He was already gone, though. As if he'd simply disappeared like some kind of magical creature.

Henry stood next to her. "Is Reece in trouble?"

"No." Lianna looked down at the keys he'd handed her. She could run away with Henry. They could disappear. He'd given her the means to escape. "I think he's trying to help us."

Henry's hand slipped into hers. "I think so, too. We should probably wait for him."

Lianna took a deep breath. Reece had given her a choice. Stay or go. Trust him or not. Knowing she had no real reason to trust him, probably knowing she didn't trust herself.

"Maybe we should."

REECE WAS SURE Sabrina wouldn't appreciate backup, but Elsie's call about what she was seeing on the cameras had made Reece nervous enough to want to make sure.

Besides, it gave Lianna a chance to make her decision without him there to muddy the Henry waters. Once they dealt with this threat, he'd find her one way or another and make sure she stayed safe.

He ran through the woods to the Bluebird, the path well enough known to him now that he didn't even stumble over the stray log or slip in the muddy earth beneath his feet.

He slowed as he reached the tree line, assessing

the situation as he approached. He didn't hear anything or see anything, so whatever was progressing must be going on inside the house. Which likely meant whoever had sent their man could hear every word.

Reece edged into the yard, scanning the area around him. Had the man really come alone? Well, why not? He likely thought he was only dealing with a woman and her child.

Unless they'd figured out who Reece was. Depending on what they'd overheard the night he'd left, it was possible they could make some assumptions. They'd have to have quite the computer guru to get to the bottom of who he was and who he worked for—but if they simply knew he wasn't who he said he was, and worked for *someone*, it was enough to potentially go in guns blazing. Depending on what they were looking for.

Reece moved forward, but stopped short when a man came sailing out of the door, crashing into the porch. The bannister held, but the man didn't. He tumbled over and fell with a thud on the damp earth below.

Sabrina followed him. She glared at Reece and flipped her dark braid over her shoulder. "I can handle one guy," she said dismissively.

Her lip was bleeding, but other than that, she'd definitely handled him. "Blame Elsie. She called me and said you might be in trouble."

Sabrina rolled her eyes. "That one. She doesn't understand a tactical display of weakness."

The man between them on the ground groaned, slowly coming to.

"What's the plan with the muscle?" Reece asked.

"I'll tie him up. Get Els on the phone and see if she got a real ID. Where's your quarry?"

"Left them with the car."

"Did you *want* them to run off?"

Reece didn't respond to Sabrina's question. As far as he was concerned, this mission might be North Star business, but Lianna and Henry were *his* assignment.

Sabrina hopped off the porch over the bannister, grinning down at the man she'd beaten. "You picked the wrong lady to screw with, you son of a—"

She was securing his hands and wrists with zip ties before the man had a chance to even attempt to roll away.

Reece dialed Elsie, who answered without a hello. "I'm working on an ID. Getting there."

"So what do we do with him?"

"Leave him. Once I get the ID, I'll send the appropriate cleanup crew. You two need to get out of there. I'm pretty sure the guy sent an SOS to his cronies. They'll be swarming the place soon as they can. Get back to headquarters. By the time you get here, I'll have more information to go on."

"Got it." Reece ended the connection. He headed for the door.

"What are you doing?" Sabrina demanded. "My bike is right there. We'll ride over to your friend."

"Locking up the place."

"You can't be serious."

"It's her home."

Sabrina rolled her eyes. "It looks so sweet and peaceful. Makes my skin crawl."

"You're a strange woman, Sabrina."

She grinned.

Reece did a quick walk-through, turning off lights and unplugging things. He grabbed a few things for Henry and Lianna—his video games, her purse.

"Ticktock," Sabrina called from outside.

Reece sighed. He dead-bolted all but the back door, but used the inside lock to secure it. It wasn't *secure*, if someone wanted to break in, but at least he'd be able to tell Lianna he'd done his best. And whatever happened, Elsie had eyes on the inn now.

He rounded the house and walked back to the front, where Sabrina was waiting on her bike. "You done playing maid?"

"Yeah, yeah," he muttered. "You really going to make me hop on the back of that thing?"

"Climb on, Montgomery. Don't be a wuss."

Frowning at the bike between her legs, Reece sighed. He'd look like an overlarge oaf on the back, but he supposed that was close enough to what he was.

He climbed on, then held on for dear life as Sabrina flew out of the yard. He had to clamp his teeth together to keep from lecturing her on safety.

She flew down the road, then over bumpy grass, cutting through a field to bypass the highway, without getting caught in the woods. As they approached where his car had been parked, Reece's stomach tensed.

Lianna had probably taken off and they'd have to track her. Well, he wasn't going to do that on the back of Sabrina's motorcycle, that was for sure.

"Looks like your friend stayed," Sabrina said over the roar of the engine.

Not my friend, he wanted to say, but he didn't. Because that wasn't the way Sabrina meant it, and it had too many uncomfortable sensations tangling with the needs of the moment.

He could see the sun glinting off the metal of his car and, as they got closer, Lianna standing in almost the exact position he'd left her. Henry still tossing the ball.

Reece felt an indescribable pressure inside him. One he couldn't deal with because they had to get to safety. They had to get to the bottom of this.

Sabrina pulled to a screeching halt in front of Lianna and Henry.

"Whoa," Henry said with clear awe as he stared at Sabrina and her motorcycle. "Are you a Valkyrie?" At Sabrina's confused stare, Henry smiled. "You know. Like in *Thor*."

Sabrina laughed. "Something like that, kid." She turned to Reece, who'd gotten off Sabrina's death trap at the first opportunity. "Well, I like him."

"Yeah, he's all right," Reece said roughly, offering Henry a smile. "Meet you at headquarters?"

Sabrina nodded. Then she glanced at Lianna. "No worries. Prince Charming over here locked up your inn. Can't promise more goons won't come, but we've got cameras on the place. He can fill you in."

Then Sabrina took off, as loudly and dangerously as she'd come.

Lianna stood stock-still, as if she'd been shocked into some kind of vegetative state. It only broke when Reece approached and spoke.

"You didn't leave," he said, his words rougher than necessary.

She blinked, then swallowed, looking down at the keys in her hand. "No, I didn't." She held the keys out to him, met his gaze. He could see trepidation in the blue depths of her eyes, but she straightened her shoulders with purpose. "I guess you should drive us to this headquarters of yours."

He blew out a breath. He didn't know what had won her over, or if it would last, but it was a step in the right direction. In the direction that would allow him to put all his effort into keeping her safe.

He took the keys, but instead of letting her drop them into his palm, he closed his hand over hers. "I'm going to do everything in my power to keep you and Henry safe. *Everything.* Whether you believe that or not, I want you to hear me say it."

She stared at him, arrested, but she didn't tug her hand away. It was small and capable in his large one.

Reece knew he was letting himself get in too deep. Even if no one else knew it, he was drowning in something he didn't understand. Didn't know how to fight, when he'd always known how to fight.

The fight was all he'd ever had.

She pulled her hand away, blinked and turned to her son. "Come on, Henry. We're going on a road trip."

Chapter Nine

Lianna dozed off as they drove, unable to keep her eyes open. She supposed it was the adrenaline wearing off.

And you clearly trust Reece way too much.

He'd locked up her inn. He worked with some… amazon woman who roared around on a motorcycle with a split lip and smoky laugh. He promised to protect her and Henry with a fierceness she didn't know how to convince herself was made up.

Every time the rough drive bumped her awake, she'd glance back at Henry. Reece had offered him his video game device, which he'd apparently swiped for Henry when he'd been locking up.

Sleep was a lot less complicated than all…that. So she let it overtake her again. The next time she woke up, the sun was setting in a riot of oranges and bright pinks in front of her. They were pulling up on some sort of circular driveway to a…

House was too subtle a word. It was more like a compound. Rustic decor, but like some high-end hunting resort rather than…

Well, whatever she assumed it actually was. "This is something else."

Reece smiled wryly.

She glanced back at Henry. His head was bent over the game, that glazed-over look in his eyes when he'd spent too much time playing. "All right. Hand it over."

"Mooooo*om*."

It was comforting that even in the midst of all *this*, Henry could maintain his epic whining skills.

"Right now."

He groaned and moaned for a few extra seconds, likely trying to finish some battle before he finally logged off the device and handed it over. He looked up grumpily, but then the frustration on his face melted away.

He flung himself forward in the car, squinting at the big house in front of them. "Whoa! You live here?"

"Not really," Reece replied. "This is where I work."

"And the Valkyrie?"

"Yeah, her too."

"Cool. Can we get out?"

Reece nodded, pushing his door open. Henry scrambled out of the car, and Lianna knew she should, too, but for a moment she was so overwhelmed by *everything* that she felt like nothing more than dead weight.

But Henry was bounding toward this strange place, and she couldn't let him be out there alone. She couldn't...

There were so many things she couldn't do, no matter how she felt. She pushed out of the car and forced her heavy legs to move.

"There's plenty of space. You and Henry will have a room. You can rest up for a while before we go over everything."

She shook her head at Reece. She'd grabbed Henry's backpack and she held the straps in a tight grip as if it would keep her centered in this strange new world. "No. I want to…" She didn't know how to complete that sentence, but Reece nodded as if he understood anyway.

He led them to the door. There were a series of security hoops to jump through. Some sort of finger-print scan, hidden behind a slab in the wooden planks of the panel next to the door. Then there was a code on the door to punch in. Henry watched it all with wide eyes, and Lianna imagined she had a similar expression on her face.

What had she gotten herself into?

Eventually, Reece put a normal-looking key in the door and the lock clicked. He pushed open the door and ushered her and Henry inside. There was a petite woman waiting for them.

"Betty," Reece greeted her.

"Hey, Reece. Shay sent me to grab bags, show room assignments."

"We want to get the important stuff out of the way first."

Betty nodded, then turned to Lianna with a smile. "I can take your bags if you'd like and put them in your room. We should be able to supply you with whatever you don't have."

"I don't have…anything. Not my purse. No clothes or… I just have my phone."

"I got your purse. And Henry's inhaler. The rest I'm sure we'll be able to supply for you temporarily," Reece said.

Lianna blinked. How would he even know to…? Where had he put…?

Betty held out her hands, and it took Lianna too long to realize she meant to take Henry's backpack. After a few more seconds of utter confusion, and the utmost patience on Betty and Reece's part, Lianna handed over the bag. Reece also handed her a backpack she hadn't realized he'd been carrying.

"You can take them to the meeting room, Reece. Shay will be available shortly," the woman said, then bustled away purposefully.

Lianna watched her go, then looked at Reece. "You all just use your real names?"

"For the most part. We don't really exist for the years we're with the group, and I didn't have much of a profile before that. It's easy to be erased, which allows us to be who we are here."

The group. Erased. It sounded ominous, but the woman who'd taken their stuff had seemed so… normal.

Reece led them down a hallway and then into a big room. It looked like some sort of meeting room with a large table and lots of chairs around it. There was a computer and monitors lining one wall. Lots of speakers and absolutely no windows.

The woman from the motorcycle earlier was already there, kicked back in a chair as if she was relaxing. She straightened when they entered. "Hey, kid." She grinned at Henry, to his clear delight.

"Hi, Valkyrie," Henry said.

"Call me Sabrina. And if it's okay with your mom, I'm going to go show you our game room."

"Like video games?"

"Yup. You ever been to an arcade?"

"You have an arcade?" Lianna asked under her breath.

Reece shrugged. "Sometimes you gotta pass the time as mindlessly as possible."

"Can I go? Can I go?" Henry demanded, clearly not at all concerned about all the strangers around them. Or the strange place and danger and…

Lianna looked up imploringly at Reece. "I'd really prefer it if he stayed with me."

"I might be able to help with that." Another woman entered the room. She looked more like the first one than Sabrina. Normal. Just an average young woman dressed in jeans and a T-shirt. But she went to a computer, tapped a few keys and then pointed to one of the many monitors along the wall.

On one monitor was the view of a room filled with arcade games. "You'll be able to keep your eyes on him. I can even turn on audio if you want."

"I…"

"Come on, Mom. Please. Please. *Please.*"

Well, she certainly didn't want him hearing anything she had to say to Reece or his…coworkers.

And this provided her no excuse. She'd be able to see and hear Henry.

And what if they do something to him? They could...

"You remember the red door we passed?" Reece asked. "In the first hallway."

"Well, yes."

"That's the arcade room."

Apparently, he could read her thoughts. Or she was *that* transparent. "Fine. All right. Just...be good, Henry. Polite." She had no idea why she was warning her son to be polite when they were in the midst of all this. Just...habit. Ridiculous, mindless habit.

"Awesome!" Henry bounced, turning his attention to Sabrina. "Can I play whatever games I want?"

"Sure thing, kid." She led him out of the room and Lianna had to curl her hands into fists to keep from panicking and running after them. She glanced at the monitor. It only took a few seconds, and then Henry raced into the room. Sabrina kicked back in the corner, giving him the run of the place.

Lianna could see everything. Hear everything.

"I'll tell Shay you're ready for her," the woman who'd brought up the room on the monitor said. She smiled at Lianna, then waited for Reece's nod before she left the room.

"Are you in charge?" Lianna asked.

"Hardly. Elsie is tech, which means she'll answer to whatever operative is handling the assignment."

"And you're handling the assignment of me."

"Yes."

"Why?"

REECE HAD NO idea how to answer that question, especially when she asked it with that baffled horror. He knew she was struggling with the decision to come with him, struggling with trusting them. Who could blame her?

She kept her eyes glued to the monitor, so Reece figured he'd give her all the truths he could.

"I'm a field operative. When an…assignment comes up, Shay determines who's going to handle it."

"Shay is your boss. The one you were talking to when you…" She trailed off but finally took her eyes off Henry on the monitor. "You said you wouldn't let a kid get caught in the cross fire. I'm holding you to that, Reece. For whatever it's worth, I'm *depending* on you and yours to keep Henry safe."

"I will."

She nodded, though he knew she didn't fully believe him. She didn't *not* believe him. She was just conflicted, and rightfully so. "Shay is in charge here. She manages the rest of us, a combination of field operatives, tech gurus and medical staff."

"You have medical staff?"

"Yes, though most of them are on call. But Betty is our head doctor. She's headquartered here and takes care of, well, anything that pops up."

"Like someone getting hurt."

"If the mission is dangerous enough. But it's not just that. We're normal people who need physicals and to be told to get some rest or eat better if we're run-down."

Lianna took some time to think over that, watching Henry's every move again.

"I'm sorry we had to bring you here. I should have…handled this better. I know Henry missing school isn't ideal, and you have an inn to run, and I promise we'll do everything to get you back home and safe as soon as possible."

Lianna nodded. "What…what happens next?"

"Elsie should have an ID on the guy at your inn today. Hopefully she can trace him to whoever placed those listening devices. From there, ideally, we can neutralize any threat against you and Henry."

Lianna looked perplexed. It wasn't fear, exactly, but still he wanted to soothe her. Assure her that North Star was the best of the best and she'd be safe. Everything would be taken care of. If he had to lay down his life to make it so.

But Shay strode in, Elsie following behind.

"Reece," Shay greeted him. "Mrs. Kade, I want to thank you for coming with us. It makes it a lot easier to keep you and your son safe with you here under our protection. At least until we understand the threat against you." Shay settled herself in her normal seat at the head of the table. Elsie sat next to her.

Normally, Reece stood for these interactions, but he thought Lianna needed to sit. She wasn't used to…any of this.

So he pulled a chair back for her and she hesitantly slid into it. He took the seat next to her.

Shay's gaze remained on Lianna. "Do you?"

"Do I what?"

"Understand the threat against you?"

"Oh, well." She slid a glance at Reece. "Reece said they must have overheard our conversation. About the listening devices. I don't understand why they'd be listening. I don't understand…any of it."

"You don't know who would put listening devices in your home?" Shay asked. Her voice was casual rather than demanding, but Reece still had to hold himself back from telling Shay to cool it.

"Not specifically," Lianna said. Her gaze darted from Shay to Elsie to Reece to the monitor. She couldn't seem to settle on any one place to look. She twisted her fingers in her lap. "Any one of the men who wanted more information about my late husband."

"Right. You understand that at this point we're concerned not just about the threat against you, minor though it's been, but what they might have overheard about *us*."

This time the look Shay gave Reece was not casual. Apparently, Shay had deduced a little bit more about his slipup than he'd hoped.

"It's just…" Lianna looked at Henry on the screen, then down at her folded hands. "I don't think they overheard things, exactly. At least, not… It's just…" Lianna blew out a breath and Reece was…confused.

This was not the woman he had come to know, however superficially. There was a timidity to her and an almost stream-of-consciousness way of speaking that wasn't Lianna at all. Even when she'd agreed to go with him, she hadn't led him to think she was lost and confused and didn't know what to say. It had been a resigned best-of-two-rotten-situations attitude.

This was different. *An act.*

"Reece mentioned the devices during a conversation, yes, and a little bit about his work. But I didn't believe him, exactly, and I told him to go. So when I went to my room that night, I... Well, I pulled the one in my room off the smoke detector. And instead of putting it back, I threw it in my desk drawer."

Reece leaned back in his chair. Well, he hadn't expected *that*. No wonder she was acting fishy. She'd tampered with the listening device.

"I suppose that was all the tip-off they needed," Shay muttered.

"Except I don't understand. For months right after Todd was killed they asked me questions. I didn't have answers. Then someone set these listening devices up, and I haven't talked about Todd beyond saying that he was killed and that I didn't know anything. Why do they think I know something?"

Shay's expression was as grim as Reece's felt. They didn't have the answers for that question. And that grated.

"Here's what we can offer, Mrs. Kade. A place to stay while we identify the man who came to your inn this afternoon."

"We're close," Elsie offered, tapping away on her computer. "I've dug through the first two fake identities. I think the real one is just within reach."

"All we need from you is your cooperation in telling us what you know about your late husband."

"I don't know anything," Lianna said, a trembling note to her voice that...

Reece had to wonder what was wrong with him. It sounded fake, and didn't inspire any of his usual sympathy or protective instincts when it came to Lianna. Instead, it made him suspicious.

You're losing it, Montgomery.

"Maybe something we find will jog a memory or two. All we're asking is that you're honest with us, and answer any of our questions to the best of your ability. It's our top priority to keep you and your son safe, but we can't promise that for good until we know who and what we're dealing with."

"How did I come to be an assignment if you don't know who or what you're dealing with?"

And *that* reminded him more of the real Lianna. A smart question, delivered in a strong voice. Determination, even if fear and worry were at the edges.

Shay leaned back in her chair, eyes narrowing as she studied Lianna. Immediately Lianna dropped her eyes and started fiddling with her hands again. "This is just so hard and I don't know… It's overwhelming." She dabbed at her eyes. Eyes that, as far as Reece could tell, were dry.

She *was* playing a part. She had to be.

"What do you know, Lianna?" he demanded, maybe a little too harshly.

Her gaze whipped up to his, and the look in her eyes did not match the fumbling, scared mask she was putting on for Shay. "What do you mean?"

"You're hiding something. You're putting on this scared, grieving widow act, but it doesn't work. I've been around you. I know this isn't you."

"A few days' stay at my inn hardly gives you leave to *know* me, Reece," she said, but it was that sharp, strong voice again. Her real backbone showing through.

Reece saw Shay and Elsie exchange a glance. They were seeing it, too. Whether they knew her or not, they'd realized she was playing the hapless widow.

"I know you're scared that whatever Todd did might touch you and Henry. I understand that. And I promise you, we all promise you, we will do everything we can to keep you and Henry safe. No matter what you know or don't. But that only works if we know what you know. You're putting us at a disadvantage if you're hiding things. We won't be able to protect you as effectively. I know you don't trust me, but you have to trust that we're working toward keeping you safe, or you wouldn't be here with Henry."

"You kidnapped me."

"You waited for me, Lianna. Please, tell us what is it you know."

Her gaze went back to Henry on the monitor. She was quiet for a few humming seconds. She wasn't twisting her fingers anymore; she had them clasped in her lap. Tightly. When she finally spoke, it was with a gravity befitting the situation and with none of the melodrama. "Everything I've done since Todd died is for my son. To keep him safe. To keep us both safe."

"You won't be in any trouble, Mrs. Kade, if that's what you're worried about. No matter what you might have done—"

"Oh, please, I haven't *done* anything," Lianna snapped. "But I do…" She trailed off and looked at

Reece, and he could read every doubt, every worry, every fear of hers in her blue eyes.

She looked for the longest time, so he held her gaze. Willing her to believe. To understand. To lay some of this burden on him instead of keeping it solely on her own shoulders.

"I do know a few things," she finally said. "Things I shouldn't."

Chapter Ten

Lianna's heart was hammering in her chest. The act that had worked so well when she'd talked to the FBI and whatever other men had come to interrogate her after Todd's death hadn't worked at all on Reece. If she wasn't totally misreading the room, Shay and Elsie hadn't bought it, either.

How had she gotten so bad at pretending? How had they seen through her?

Why are you going to tell them?

The truth was… She didn't know how to keep Henry safe now. Not with listening devices and strange men in her inn. She thought she'd won, but she hadn't. Not fully.

And despite all the ways her brain told her not to ever trust anyone again, she couldn't help believing Reece and his "group" would keep her safe. They'd been too kind. They'd bent over backward to make her feel comfortable, to give Henry something fun to do. To give her the space to make her own choices, such as they were.

Reece had played *catch* with Henry. Sabrina was currently battling him in some arcade game and they were both laughing. Shay, Elsie and Reece were all looking at her expectantly, but they weren't demanding immediate answers.

She had no other choice now. She'd thought maybe she could get the protection without the cooperation, and maybe if it had just been Reece, she would have been able to do it. Maybe. But Shay was not going to be swayed by fake tears.

Reece didn't buy your fake tears, either.

"Todd's real name," she croaked, telling them what she'd never told another living soul. "I know it."

The entire room was silent except for the crackling audio of Sabrina and Henry laughing over a game.

"All right," Shay said very carefully. "That information will go a long way in helping us sort out our next steps."

But she didn't ask, and she didn't demand. She waited.

Lianna didn't know why it felt as though that cracked her wide open. She didn't know why it made her want to confess everything right there. Or maybe grab on to Reece and cry into his very broad shoulders. She wanted, desperately, to fall apart in the way she hadn't allowed herself to this whole hellish year.

Instead, she swallowed down all those wants, all that pain and all that fear. It took her longer than she would have liked to fight back the tide. But she did it.

Then Reece's hand slid over her clasped ones in her lap. Big, rough, warm and gentle. There was no pressure here. This was support, because the table between them and Shay hid the action.

Though Lianna wasn't convinced Shay didn't see it or sense it or *something*. The woman was unnervingly perceptive.

Did it matter what she saw? It didn't mean anything. Nice as Reece was, sort-of kidnapping aside, she was his mission. His assignment.

Which reminded her she had her own mission. Keeping her child safe. She believed these people could help her. She had to believe that.

If they didn't, if they turned out to be bad, she'd find a way to get Henry out and to safety. She just would. This was a calculated risk, and she could mitigate it, even in telling them, if she never relaxed, never fully believed. If she was always waiting for the other shoe to fall.

Do you want to live that way?

No, of course she didn't. But Todd hadn't left her a choice in that matter.

"Charles Jackson. That's his real name, or the name the FBI think is his real one. Todd Kade was the identity I knew. He may have had more, but… I don't think he did."

"Why not?"

There was no way to lie about this and expect help. Not this deep. She had to be completely honest. "I didn't know Todd's real name, or that he even had a real name, while we were married. I was fooled, completely. I never suspected…whatever this is. It was only after he died, the way people kept asking about him, that I began to realize something wasn't right. And the more I was questioned, the more I started to piece together Todd's lies."

"So how did you find out his real name if he didn't tell you while he was alive?"

It was Shay asking the questions, but it was Reece with his hand on hers. He hadn't pulled it away, and for some reason that settled her, helped her call upon the inner strength she'd had to build since Todd's death.

So when she spoke, she spoke to Reece. "At first, when the police came and told me Todd had been killed, their questions were... It didn't make it sound like a burglary. They asked if I knew anyone who might have hurt him or had been threatening him. They thought it was a purposeful, specific-to-him murder in those early hours."

She didn't want to relive those awful hours. That spurt of relief, even as the questions had left her more confused than anything. Then telling Henry...

She wanted to remember none of what had happened in San Francisco.

"She gave us the name," Reece said to Shay. "Isn't that enough for now? It's been a long day for her."

Lianna straightened and shook her head. "No, I want to get it all out. It's hard to... I've never told anyone this. Not anyone. Not Henry, not my parents or grandparents. I kept it all to myself. Always. So it's hard to...undo that. Keeping it locked down has kept us safe."

"I understand," Shay said. "Take your time, Mrs. Kade."

Lianna winced. "Please stop calling me that. Just Lianna is fine. And *I'm* fine," she said to Reece. She took a deep breath and slowly let it out. "Then the

FBI got involved. They mentioned that Todd might be involved in something. They asked me questions and I was legitimately in the dark. They seemed to believe me. But day after day, week after week, more men came. At first I thought they were all FBI, but then…" She told herself she'd kept this secret because it had kept her safe, but as an embarrassed flush worked its way up her neck, she realized part of her was trying to save face. Trying to hide how utterly stupid she'd been.

Because it hadn't just been Todd lying to her. She'd believed every man in a suit who'd come to her door with questions. She'd answered them all, never suspecting anything. Until…

"I moved to Denver, to my parents' house. My grandparents came to stay with us, too. I thought that would be the end of it. Here I am home. Surrounded by family. Then an FBI agent there wanted to talk to me. Tie up loose ends, he said." She looked up at Shay. "He wanted me to meet him at a coffee shop, and it took me all that time to realize some of these men—the ones *not* meeting me at their FBI offices—clearly weren't FBI. That's when I knew I couldn't just say I didn't know. I had to act as stupid and inept as possible so they'd *believe* it."

"Let me guess," Elsie muttered. "The men fell for it hook, line and sinker."

Lianna chuckled, though it felt bitter in her throat. "Yeah, the stupider I acted, the less they bothered me. But I thought… I thought the FBI should know that other men were questioning me. I knew Todd was… Well, that he wasn't involved in good things.

I thought maybe the FBI would be able to figure it out and what I told them might help. But I'd been playing stupid for so long, they didn't really believe me. Oh, they took the meeting, asked a few perfunctory questions, but that was it. Except they had gotten out Todd's file."

"Like a paper file?" Shay asked.

Lianna nodded. "It was sitting there between us. Labeled 'Charles Jackson.' And I didn't have a clue who Charles Jackson was at that point. I just figured he grabbed the wrong file because he was that bored. Then he opens it, and there's Todd's picture. That's when it dawned on me."

"Did you say anything?" Reece asked.

Lianna shook her head. "I kept waiting for him to…say something about it. Or act weird. Or anything. But he was bored. Flipped through a few pages. I didn't react. I tried not to look once I figured it out. I didn't want to know. Or knew I shouldn't know, but I saw some things."

"Like?"

"His real birth date, three years before he'd told me his was. That he was born in Michigan, not Wyoming."

Elsie was already tapping away on her computer. "That's a lot to go on, Mrs.—er, Lianna. A *lot*."

Shay nodded, clearly surprised that Lianna had been able to give them so much. Lianna knew she could leave it at that. With a name and a birth date they could maybe figure some things out.

But she knew more. More that might point them

in the right direction. She'd decided to be honest. No point in holding back now. "I'm not…finished."

"You know *more*?" Shay asked, the unflappable woman seeming a little bit…flapped.

"There was a list of groups they'd connected Todd to. I didn't see the full list, but I saw two of the names. And I remember them."

REECE PULLED HIS hand away. Clearly Lianna didn't need his support. Hell, she'd have been better off if he'd never crashed into her life.

She knew all this. But had never told a soul.

Reece slid a look at Shay. *Flabbergasted* was the only word he could use to describe it. Then her eyes narrowed and met his.

Still, her voice was mild when she spoke. "What were the groups' names?"

"One was Ripe for Execution."

"Oh, brother," Elsie muttered under her breath.

"The other was a series of letters and numbers. I can't be sure I remembered them in the right order, but the letters were definitely *T* and *K*, and the numbers were 29. I only remember because it was his initials and his birthday—at least the ones he told me. Not his real ones."

"That's excellent," Shay said, leaning back in her chair. "Much more than I expected. Thank you. Is there anything else?"

Lianna shook her head. "No. Not that I can think of."

"We'll likely have some questions for you once

we investigate on our end, but for now, why don't you go get some rest?"

"Oh. Well. I... Henry's probably starving. We usually have a snack after the bus, and dinner by—"

"We'll get that all sorted out." Shay stood and walked over to the door, opening it to reveal Betty. "Can you show Mrs.—Lianna to the kitchen? Give her a tour, see if she has any special requests?"

"Sure," Betty said, giving Lianna a friendly smile.

Reece stood. No need to push all that off onto Betty just because there weren't any medical concerns right now. "We've got a whole gym set up in the basement if Henry gets restless. Why don't I—"

"Sit, Montgomery. We have a lot of things to discuss," Shay said sharply.

Lianna looked back at him, eyes wide. So, despite his sense of impending doom, he smiled. "A few formalities. I'll catch up with you and Henry soon."

Lianna looked at Shay, then back to him, then Betty. She sighed, clearly understanding there was nothing she could do here. She followed Betty into the hallway.

Shay closed the door behind them. Reece didn't sit. Maybe it was petty, but he wouldn't sit for the dressing-down he was about to get.

"What I'd like to know is why this woman has a good chunk of the answers we're looking for and you spent a week with her and didn't have a clue." Shay crossed her arms over her chest and leaned against the door behind her.

Reece stood, posture rigid, feeling a bit like he

was back in the military, without the salute. "She told you. She didn't share that with anyone."

"Yeah, your job is to be better than *anyone*. That's why we sent you to her inn, Reece. I don't like knowing you kept things from us."

"I didn't…" No point lying. He'd done what he'd done because he thought it was the right way to handle things. "Look, I had a little slipup. I was fixing things."

"Hardly." Shay pushed off the door. "You're off this one."

"What?" Reece demanded, stepping forward without fully realizing he was doing it. "You can't do that."

Shay opened the door and was already stepping out of the room. "I can and I will. Sabrina and Holden will handle her from here on out. You stay out of it. I'll get you a new assignment." She started to leave, muttering about how she'd like to send him to Alaska.

Reece had been a member of North Star for over six years now. He had never once ignored or argued with an order. He'd certainly never outright refused one. "No," he said firmly, and perhaps with a little too much volume.

He could feel Elsie's eyes on him rather than on the computer like they were supposed to be.

Shay stood stock-still, her back to him. She took a very slow, deep breath before she stepped back in the room and calmly closed the door and turned to face him. Her expression was *not* calm, but her voice was controlled, if icy. "You took an oath when you

signed on to North Star, and part of that oath was
following orders."

"To Granger Macmillan."

She blinked, the only clue that the statement had
hit its mark. "Two years, Reece. Don't try to play this
off as some sort of misplaced loyalty to Macmillan.
I've been in charge for two years, and you haven't
disobeyed an order the entire time."

"I haven't felt the need."

"You shouldn't feel the need now. Your loyalty is
to North Star, not a woman you just met. If this is
some sort of…"

"Let's not pretend you, of all people, can lecture
me on following orders to the letter regardless of
personal feelings."

Shay cocked her head, and this time her surprise
was written all over her face. That he'd dare mention
the fact she'd gone her own way, against Granger's
clear orders, and more than once.

"You're right. When I was in your position, I
stayed true to what I knew was right when Granger
had lost track of it. What was *right*, Montgomery.
Not my own personal feelings."

"Yeah, well, this is *my* right." But he wasn't handling it very well, and that grated. He'd never…
not handled things. He'd never been out of control
or made decisions because of *emotion*. He wished
he could back down having realized that. But he
couldn't.

"Lianna and Henry are my responsibility. You
won't take me off this mission."

Shay's eyebrows drew together as she studied him. "Is there something you're not telling me?"

"No."

She sighed and then rubbed her hand over her face. Exhaustion seemed to line her expression and Reece felt…guilty. He'd always believed in the party line. In following orders. In letting the leaders lead.

But he didn't know how to sit back and let Sabrina and Holden handle this when he…when he… "I just care, okay? About them specifically."

"After a few days?" Shay asked skeptically.

Warranted skepticism. Understandable skepticism. A skepticism he wished he could access. But all he had were these feelings inside of him he couldn't reason away. "Yeah, after a few days."

"Caring about someone can be a dangerous liability on an assignment. Trust me."

"Dangerous liability or not, would you ever let someone else handle something that involved people you cared about?"

Shay didn't answer that question, but the twisted expression on her face was all the answer Reece needed.

"Fine," Shay said at last. "You're still lead. But you *have* to keep us in the loop. Slipups or no. Anything she tells you, you have to tell us. It's the only way it works. It's the only way we end this for them."

"Even if this group who's hired us turns out to want to hurt them?"

"*Especially* then. North Star won't be used to hurt people," she said vehemently. "Not as long as I'm in charge."

"All right. I'm going to go help them with dinner." He turned to Elsie. "I want whatever you find, whenever you find it. Everything on him, on those groups, no matter how inconsequential."

Elsie's lips twitched. "Sure thing, boss."

"I'm not the boss," he muttered, stalking away from her and past Shay.

"Remember that, huh?" Shay called after him, but she smiled at him, making it clear she was sort of joking.

Which was a nice way to end things that had been tense there for a minute. But he'd said things he maybe shouldn't have, or at least shouldn't have used as weapons. He didn't want to let that sit on his conscience. "For what it's worth, you've done a hell of a job since Granger. I haven't doubted you once, and I doubted him a time or two."

Shay stood completely still, as if shocked by his words. Hell, she probably was. He wasn't one for compliments or any sort of heart-to-hearts. Admitting he cared about Lianna and Henry and then telling her she was a good leader were two very un-Reece-like things to do in a short period of time.

But eventually she nodded. "Thanks. Now let's wrap this up so your friends can go home."

It was Reece's turn to nod and walk away, and try not to think too deeply about this being over, with Lianna and Henry back home and Reece...

Here. Alone.

Just like you were meant to be.

Chapter Eleven

The kitchen was overwhelming. About three times the size of her kitchen at the inn, and twice as stocked.

Betty was a kind, quiet soul. Lianna couldn't figure out how she fit in around here, but she was grateful for her calming presence as she showed them their options for food.

"Why is everything so healthy?" Henry whined.

Betty chuckled even as Lianna was embarrassed Henry would complain about free food and free safety.

"We do keep it pretty healthy around here, but I have the makings for a PB and J or a grilled cheese."

"You really don't have to. I can make food for us. It doesn't feel right having you fuss over us when…" Lianna trailed off, not sure how to put to words what this whole situation was.

"I know it must feel awkward, especially since you've been pulled into something against your will, but the whole purpose of this place is to help. That's why we're here. Whether that means out in the field or making a grilled cheese."

Reece appeared in the kitchen, so quietly Lianna nearly jumped. Her heart thumped against her chest and she told herself it was nerves. Now he knew everything. Now what would happen?

But there was a flutter in her chest, underneath all that thumping, which spoke of a completely different feeling than nerves and worry.

"I can take it from here, Bet."

Betty nodded at Reece. "I'm around for the next few days. Let me know if you need anything."

"Thank you. Really. I…"

Betty waved her off, then slid out of the kitchen almost as quietly as Reece had entered.

"Are you gonna have grilled cheese, too, Reece?" Henry asked, trying to peek into the pantry without Lianna noticing.

"That sounds good. Why don't I handle dinner?"

"But…" Lianna didn't know how to argue when she didn't know where anything in the kitchen was, but she was the innkeeper. Even without the inn, she was just used to being the one who made the dinners and handled things.

Reece ushered her over to a large table. "Sit. Relax. Much as you can, anyway." He patted her shoulder in a casual manner, then went about gathering tools and ingredients.

Henry sat, but then immediately popped out of his chair to hover around Reece. Lianna didn't have the energy to scold him, and Reece handled it all deftly anyway, melting butter in a pan and taking out slices of cheese to put on pieces of bread.

"How come you don't live here? I'd love to live in a place with an arcade. I'd play *Street Fighter* every day. I'd have all the high scores."

"Lofty goals," Reece replied. "But video games get a little boring after a while, don't they?"

Henry made a scoffing noise, then wiggled his way back to her at the table. "How come we're at Rcccc's work, Mom?"

Lianna looked at her son and found herself completely and utterly at a loss for words, when usually she had a plan in place. Words to say to assure Henry everything was fine and she was handling it.

"Is it about Dad?" he asked, looking at his shoe as he kicked it against the table leg. *Tap. Tap. Tap.*

She didn't want to lie to Henry. Omission was one thing. Lying… She looked up at Reece. He was watching her, and as much as she would love for someone else to swoop in and lie to her son for her, she could tell he wasn't going to do that.

"Yes, it is." She'd never flat-out told Henry that his father was not a good man. What would be the point? Henry hadn't seen much of Todd—Todd had made sure of that—and Lianna figured Henry knew enough to know Todd hadn't been, well, *there*.

But it didn't feel right to say, *Hey, your dad was a bad man involved with bad things, and now we're paying the price*. Not to a child who was seven. So she had to choose her words very, very carefully.

"There are some men who want to know some things about your father. They think I know. So Reece is just helping us explain to them that I don't know anything."

Henry's eyebrows drew together and his gaze didn't leave his kicking foot. "Are they bad men?"

"We can't control what other people are," Lianna

said sternly. "We have to focus on who we are and how we can be good people. And if we…need some help, we can't be afraid to ask for it."

Reece moved over, sliding a plate in front of Henry and then her. Grilled cheese, some grapes and some baby carrots.

After everything today, somehow *that* was the thing that put her closest to tears.

But Reece wasn't done. He crouched next to Henry's chair and looked the boy right in the eye. "Do you trust me?"

Henry nodded.

"I know you have a lot of questions, and you should. You're a smart kid. But it's a lot of complicated adult stuff. The bottom line is I'm going to keep you and your mom safe here until we can convince these men to leave your mom alone. So there's nothing to be afraid of. Because your mom and I are handling it."

Henry stared at Reece for a few more seconds, seemingly searching the man's rugged face for… something. Lianna felt herself searching for something, too, and she was just as in the dark about what she wanted to find as Henry seemed to be.

Eventually Henry nodded. "Okay," he said. Then he smiled crookedly. "It'd probably help me to play more *Street Fighter.*"

Henry had always been a give-him-an-inch-he'll-take-a-mile type. But he was so dang cute it was hard to be stern about it. Reece laughed and glanced at Lianna, who couldn't help smiling in return. Their eyes met and…

Her stomach swooped, and there was no pretending that the flutter wasn't all those things she'd promised herself she would never allow in her life again.

But she would not listen to attraction. She would not indulge in conspiratorial smiles. For Henry, she would just shut that feminine side of her off.

Apparently, around Reece Conrad—no, Reece Montgomery—her feminine side wasn't listening to her brain...because it was too busy noticing Reece. The way his eyes crinkled when he smiled, the warmth in those dark eyes, the easy way he rested his very large hand on the back of Henry's chair.

After having made grilled cheese for all of them.

Henry dived into his dinner. Lianna picked at hers. She knew she should eat, but her stomach wasn't cooperating. Too much fear, too much worry, and sadly, not just over the current predicament. Reece was turning into his own predicament. Especially when he took a seat at the table with them with his own plate—a turkey sandwich rather than grilled cheese. He talked baseball with Henry as if this was...

Well, all the things it could never be.

After dinner, and a little bit more *Street Fighter*, Reece showed Lianna to the room she would share with Henry.

"I figured you wouldn't want separate rooms."

She smiled at him, trying to strike the right balance between polite and grateful and not give away any of that...inappropriate, untimely *fluttering.* "You figured right."

Something beeped and he pulled out his phone, frowning at it. "Looks like Elsie got a hit on some things. Do you want to meet me in the conference room once Henry's asleep, or do you want to wait?"

"I'll meet you there. I assume there's some way I can watch him from anywhere in this place?"

Reece's mouth curved wryly. "*You* assume right. Take your time. I promise I'll fill you in once he's in bed."

Lianna nodded and then Reece disappeared. He was much…quieter here. She figured it was instinct or habit. One he'd purposefully broken when he was staying with her. Whether to put her at ease or to act more like your average civilian, she had no idea, but his footsteps had been heavy. She'd mostly known when he was about. Here it was all…appearing and disappearing and… Well, she supposed what he was. An *operative*.

She went into the bathroom, found the toiletries Reece had said would be available to them and made Henry brush his teeth. They'd even thought to provide clothes. An oversize T-shirt for Henry, and what looked like women's sweats for her.

She didn't change, but she had Henry change and brush his teeth. He crawled into the bed without much argument, which was how she knew he was beyond exhausted. She sat on the edge of the bed and ran her hand over his hair. "Get a good night's sleep, baby. Lots of fighting games await you in the morning."

Henry smiled, but his eyes were already drooping. "When can we go home?" he asked around a yawn.

Lianna closed her eyes against a wave of pain and guilt. "I'm not sure, sweetheart." She wondered if she'd ever be sure about anything ever again.

"WE'VE GOT TROUBLE," Elsie said with no preamble when Reece strode through the door. "Major trouble."

"How?"

"I started digging into Charles Jackson, right? Well, everyone and their brother has a flag on the guy's record. Got around the FBI and a few other groups I didn't take the time to identify yet, no problem, but one group had their flag hidden."

Reece didn't know much about computers, but he knew that meant... "So someone knows we're looking for Charles Jackson."

"They don't know who or where we are. I have protections against that. But they know someone is looking, and it doesn't take a leap of reason to realize that if someone just happened to start looking into him today..."

"They know Lianna told us his name."

"Or they're at least going to make that assumption," Elsie confirmed.

Reece swore. Instead of getting her out of trouble, they'd put her smack down into the middle of it. They'd made her a target, not just a questionable liability.

He swore again.

"I take full responsibility," Elsie said, her voice quavering just a hair. "It's completely my fault. I didn't see the flag. I've never seen one like that. This is my fail."

"Or they're that good. Sometimes the wrong people get the best of us, Els," Reece said with more calm and graciousness than he felt. Elsie was young.

She wasn't an operative. Tech geniuses couldn't be expected to handle everything. "Now we just have to make sure we take the next step first and best."

"I'm not handing any of this off to my other tech people. I'm going to take extra precautions before I look into the names of the groups she gave us. But it'll take longer."

"Then it'll take longer. We don't want to rush into anything."

Shay strode into the room. "I agree. No targets on anyone's head. Unfortunately, you're going to have to break it to Mrs. Kade so she understands how important it is for her and her son to stay here for the time being."

"I don't think she's under the illusion she'd be safer at the inn," Reece returned stiffly. Better stiff than furious. Better closed off than let go of all the anger building inside of him.

"You never know," Shay replied with a shrug that grated on Reece's frayed temper.

"We should send an operative to each group," he said through gritted teeth. "Including the FBI. Who knows how they're involved?"

Shay shook her head and Reece had to curl his fingers into fists to keep from demanding to know why.

"I just spoke to my contact, the one who brought this little assignment to our doorstep. I told him we'd found some information, but that I needed more on his end to share it. Eventually, he gave me a little more to go on."

"FBI?" Elsie asked.

"No. A group called T2K9."

Elsie frowned at her computer screen. "That was one of the groups Lianna told us about that was on the FBI file. So they're bad?"

"Not exactly. After some circular arguments, and calling in a favor from Granger, I was given enough information to believe they actually are one of the good guys."

"You talked to Granger?" Elsie asked, wide-eyed. "I thought he wouldn't talk to anyone."

"He makes the occasional exception. Mostly when I threaten him with all of us invading his little ranch or whatever he's calling it these days. Besides, it was just information. Information he had."

"Did they plant the devices?" Reece demanded. Much as he cared about his former boss and his recluse act, now was not the time to dwell on it. Reece needed to know more before he agreed with Shay's assessment that the group that had approached them wasn't going to hurt Lianna—whether on purpose or collaterally.

"No. They didn't. Apparently Todd Kade was a member, under the name Jack Charles, so Lianna was wrong about him not having any other names. T2K9 discovered he was playing them shortly before he died. They made the connection to the Todd Kade identity, and knew they needed more information. They couldn't find it, so they came to us. You won't be surprised to know the head guy over there knew Granger and enough about us to think we'd be able to find what they couldn't."

"I don't understand. How was this one guy involved in so much?" Reece demanded.

"Charles Jackson liked to spread his talents around. He's got links to more than just the groups Mrs. Kade gave us. Good, bad, questionable. It's not clear why or how."

"Jack Charles was an FBI informant," Elsie said, typing away at her computer. "There aren't any flags, hidden or otherwise, on that name. I can dig up all sorts of things on him."

"That explains the FBI's involvement," Shay said, leaning over Elsie's shoulder to look at the monitor.

"So which of these groups put out the listening devices?" Reece demanded, irritated that the two women seemed more interested in what one man had done than what certain men were *currently* doing. "Who sent the man?"

"We're still working on those answers."

"Damn it, Shay, that's not good enough," Reece said, and though he kept his voice controlled, it was an outburst all the same.

One he immediately regretted when he turned and saw Lianna standing in the doorway, hands clasped together. Her expression was carefully neutral, but she held herself so very still.

He wished he could reason out the emotion that slammed through him every time he looked at her, and that it was never quite the same, but always... deep, immediate. Troubling.

He didn't know what it was, and he couldn't fight it. He could only stand there while she looked at him with wide, scared eyes.

"It seems things are a little more tense than they were an hour ago," she finally said when no one spoke. And there was no stutter, no tremor of fear. Her voice was perfectly calm and steady.

Because for a year now, she'd faced down this uncertainty and had to put on a brave face for Henry. She was a strong woman, made stronger by a circumstance beyond her control.

And Reece had to stop worrying about stupid feelings plaguing him and focus on giving her what she really needed—safety and peace of mind. This problem erased so she and Henry could have a normal life.

"We've got a few leads," Shay said. "Unfortunately, the people who want information from you are a little more…underhanded than we might have anticipated. It's very possible they know you've given us a name."

Lianna's face paled, but she raised her chin. "How would that have happened?"

"My fault," Elsie said, and her tone was both professional and apologetic. A fine line somewhere between a human courtesy and maybe some real guilt. But Reece could also detect confidence that she could still handle the mission in front of her. "In layman's terms, they hid what amounted to a tracking device on the name Charles Jackson."

"Which means *they* know his real name," Lianna said. "Whoever these people targeting me are."

Shay nodded. "Yes. It appears Todd had a few aliases, worked for a number of groups. He couldn't have been home much."

Lianna's shoulders straightened almost imperceptibly, as if she'd taken Shay's observation as a personal insult. "He told me he was a salesman who traveled a lot. We had a baby ten months after we were married and Todd made it clear he wasn't interested in fatherhood. His trips increasing in frequency and length made sense in how much he didn't want to be around to be a father."

"No one's saying you could have known what he was," Reece offered, understanding what she considered to be an insult now.

"Aren't they?" Lianna returned with an arch look at Shay.

Shay's mouth curved. Not a patronizing smile. More of respect at a point earned. "It's not my job to make insinuations or interpret what you should have known or not, Lianna. I'm collecting observations."

Lianna made a scoffing sound. "Observations you have to weave together to form some kind of hypothesis. Some kind of mission. I didn't know what he was. I've told you everything I know, and you know what? I regret it. Because I'm apparently now in even more danger."

Shay's expression didn't change, but Reece knew her well enough to know Lianna had landed her blow. Shay nodded almost imperceptibly.

"You'll be safe here. For as long as it takes. I promise you that."

Lianna shook her head. "We can't stay here forever." She wrapped her arms around herself, eyebrows drawing together. "If we don't know who's after me. If we don't know why. If we don't know anything, that means we—"

"It means *I* will handle it," Reece said firmly.

"We'll send an operative to each group we've got. We'll get what we can out of the FBI—surely they know more than they're letting on. We'll—"

"We'll remember that *I'm* in charge here," Shay interrupted.

"With all due respect, and the understanding I'm just a civilian with no understanding of all…this," Lianna said calmly, but her nerves finally betrayed her as her hands shook before she shoved them into the pockets of her jeans. "The only way to find out who's after me is to let them come after me."

"Not a chance," Reece said, unaware those words had come out of his mouth until he realized all three women's surprised gazes were on him. Still, he didn't back down. "We're not letting an untrained civilian act as *bait* to a group we know nothing about. End of story."

"No, it's not 'end of story,'" Lianna retorted with a barely leashed fury that surprised him. "You are not in charge of me, Reece. None of you are in charge of me. I have run or hid for a year now, and I'm not any closer to safety. Henry's life is disrupted once again. It has to stop, and if I have to be the one to stop it, so be it."

Chapter Twelve

"Lianna." Shay's voice, kind and patient, made Lianna want to haul off and punch something. Particularly Reece's handsome face.

"I understand you're frustrated," Shay continued. "But like you said, you're just a civilian. You can't—"

"So train me. Help me. I don't care what you have to do. This has to end. And we all know, thanks to Todd or Charles or whatever the hell his name really was, I'm at the center. I'm the thing they're worried about or... I don't even know what they want from me, and neither do you. We won't find out without *me*."

Lianna tried to pretend that didn't scare her. Tried to brave her way through this like she'd braved her way through the past year. She liked to think she succeeded. Oh, inside she was a petrified mess, but on the outside she appeared certain. Impassioned.

She hoped.

"I'm sorry. No. We're not considering this," Reece said, more to Shay and Elsie than to her.

She couldn't say she was surprised Reece didn't

like the idea, but she was surprised at the...immensity of his conviction. Vehemence pumped off him, barely restrained. He'd begun to pace, something she'd never seen him do.

He'd always been kind and gentle and contained. Even when he'd picked her up and carried her to his car. He'd been certain and determined but not...

Impassioned.

"Lianna." Reece's entire demeanor changed. He took a deep breath and then spoke to her in a calm, authoritative manner. "You've had a long day. You should rest. We'll handle all this, since it's our fault you're a target in the first place."

Maybe he'd transferred his fury to her, because it leaped up, hot and reckless. "You will not dismiss me."

"That's not—"

"That's exactly what you're trying to do. And sure, if you want to point fingers, your little group holds some of the blame, but my home was *bugged*. Clearly whatever Todd was involved in wasn't done with me yet, even if they'd let me be. That isn't your fault. It's Todd's."

"How do you know they wouldn't have given up after enough time of not getting any information they wanted?"

"How do you know they would?"

His jaw tightened, and he adopted that preternaturally still posture that might have poked some holes in her determination if she wasn't so mad.

"I've protected myself and my son for a year. Without you," she said to Reece. "Without you," she said, pointing to Shay and Elsie. "I need help, yes, but I don't need some mysterious group sweeping in and blowing up my life, no matter how nice you all might be. You can't take away my free will. You can't tell me what to do. You are *not* in charge of me."

The room went silent. She would have categorized Reece's silence as *tense*, at best, but Shay and Elsie weren't tense so much as…curious. They both gazed at Reece as if they'd never seen him before.

Lianna didn't know how to read into that. She supposed it was beside the point anyway. "They now know I know Todd's real name. But they knew it to begin with, so they want more than that from me."

"Elsie is working on finding the real ID for the man who came to your inn this afternoon," Reece said. Through clenched teeth. He didn't have his fists bunched, but she felt that kind of tension from him anyway. As if he was ready to physically fight his way through this but was holding himself back.

"That's good," Lianna said, finding the more she observed the bubbling ferocity beneath Reece's controlled facade, the more controlled she felt. Sort of like when Henry was throwing a tantrum. She wanted to laugh at the comparison, but unlike a child's tantrum, she didn't think Reece would handle her laughing in a petulant or dismissive way.

"There are definitely some blocks. Someone doesn't want us to know who he really is or who he's connected to. I'll be able to unearth it," Elsie said, with a kind of quiet confidence that helped ease some of Lianna's fears. "It just might take more time than I'd like."

"What happens when you unearth it?" Lianna asked, with none of the snap or demand she'd had earlier. No, she was too tired for that. She was too... fed up with half answers that didn't actually *end* what Todd had brought to her doorstep. "You know the name of the group who Todd was potentially working for. But you don't know what they want from me. We won't know what they're after unless we give them some access."

"They will get *no* access to you, and that's it," Reece said. His voice was controlled, but nothing else about him was. He shocked her completely when he said no more and just stormed out of the room.

"Well, *that* was interesting," Shay murmured.

"I was laboring under the assumption Reece was a robot," Elsie said, sounding awed. "*That* was not robotic."

Both women turned their gazes to her. As if she understood...any of what they were saying or getting at.

"I...wouldn't know. I've only just met him."

"And made quite an impression. Reece has dealt with a lot more complicated, dangerous missions than this," Shay said.

"Seriously. He single-handedly saved all those guys in Afghanistan," Elsie said, though she'd turned back to her computer and was tapping away again. Trying to find the man who'd wanted to check in to her inn.

"And came out with barely a scratch when he saved that girl from, what was it, ten Sons members?"

Elsie nodded. "Then he came back and shrugged

it off as nothing and asked for the next mission." Elsie slid a look at Lianna. "And did *not* storm out of any rooms."

"Ever. I've been here longer than him. I have *never* seen him act even a little bit like that."

"I don't know what either of you are getting at," Lianna said, trying to ignore the odd flutter of… something in her chest.

"Just observations." There was some humor in Shay's expression, but it slowly melted away. "Putting yourself in harm's way is a dangerous proposition, Lianna. Even with our help. You're risking your life."

Lianna rubbed at her chest, where that nice, if alarming, flutter had turned into a jerky, beating panic. "I don't want to risk my life. But I don't want to live in fear. Henry is missing school. If this goes on much longer, he'll miss baseball. If we have to move again…" She shook her head. "He deserves a childhood. In one place. He deserves more than this. I don't know how else to give it to him."

Shay nodded. "Can you give us some time? We can plan something. Use a team. Protect you, as much as we can."

Lianna didn't understand these people. What they were getting out of it. Why they'd swooped into her life and upended everything. And worse, why she trusted them. "Why? You don't know me from Adam. I can't pay you. Why would you help me?"

"It's what we do. Protect innocent people."

She thought of Reece's story about his parents, and how his records had backed all that up. Being taken away by the state. No one had protected him growing up. Were they all like that? "Because you were once innocent people who weren't protected?"

Shay shared a look with Elsie, then turned back to Lianna. "That's exactly why," she said, firmly. Vehemently. Like it wasn't just the truth, but an oath she'd taken.

"I'll take whatever help you can give me," Lianna said in return. "Whatever protection you can give me. I don't have a death wish here. I only want it over so I can give my son the life he deserves. I think I have to put myself in a little danger to do that, but I'll absolutely wait for you guys to mitigate the level of danger I have to step into."

Shay's mouth curved. "Reece's reaction is starting to make more sense."

Lianna blinked, irritated at the heat rushing into her cheeks. She couldn't think of a thing to say.

"It's late," Shay said, with a gentleness Lianna hadn't seen from her this whole time. "Why don't you get some rest? We'll reconvene in the morning and brainstorm how this is going to work."

Lianna didn't know how she was going to sleep in this strange place, with so much worry and anxiety filling up her mind. How could anyone sleep knowing their life could be in danger? Or even just completely upended—again?

And if she worried about that, she didn't have to think about how she felt toward Reece. A stranger. Someone she barely knew but… She'd been foolish once. She'd fallen for Todd, let her heart sweep her away, because she'd chased a stupid emotion that had turned out to be fake. Fabricated.

She wouldn't do that again. Not to Henry and not to herself. Maybe she'd come to trust Reece when it came to helping her, but that didn't mean she could trust this…flutter inside of her. She *couldn't* trust it. Wouldn't.

But as she walked back to the room she'd be sleeping in, she stopped short at the entrance to the hallway. Reece was pacing agitatedly in the hallway outside the door where Henry slept. He looked a little wild, and that should put her off. It should scare her.

But it didn't. She wanted to soothe him. She wanted…him. She just needed to work on convincing herself she couldn't trust those feelings. Not so quickly. Not when her own judgment had already failed her.

Reece was nothing like Todd, but that didn't change who *she* was. The mistakes *she'd* made. In the end, the only thing that could matter was making sure Henry was safe.

Forever.

Reece paced the hallway outside the room where Henry was fast asleep. He knew he had to get control of his emotions before he spoke to Lianna, but he also knew he had to speak to her tonight before Shay and Elsie ran with any ideas of using Lianna as bait.

He couldn't stand the thought of it. It made his insides feel like rock, and like he wanted to punch his way through…well, the wall.

He hadn't felt this way in a very long time, and

he didn't revel in the return of that raging storm. In fact, it only made him *more* unsettled. Which wasn't productive. At all.

He sensed movement at the end of the hall and looked up to see Lianna standing there. She stared at him the longest time, some internal conflict going on behind her eyes, before she started toward him.

He didn't say anything as she approached. The words just…left him, and he knew he didn't have the handle on his inner turmoil or his worry to keep a lid on things that needed to stay completely buried.

"We came to an agreement," Lianna said coolly. "If you'd stayed, you might have heard it."

"If I'd stayed, I would have punched a hole in a wall," he muttered.

If she seemed surprised by that response, she didn't show it. "That's hardly constructive," she said, and she sounded like she did when she was scolding Henry.

It didn't do a lot for his temper. "I don't find myself feeling particularly constructive. I don't find myself…" He sucked in a breath, calling on all his training—as a soldier, as an operative, hell, as a foster kid who couldn't make trouble without severe consequences—and pushed down his turmoil.

Unfortunately, that left room for all those *other* feelings to take hold. Her standing there looking so… put-together, even as he could see the worry around the edges. The way her blue eyes regarded him with a wariness she *should* have, but he didn't want.

Her honey-blond hair had fallen out of its ponytail, and despite her rigid posture, she looked like a woman who'd been through hell. And he wanted…

God, the things he wanted that didn't make sense to him. He clutched at his shirt, frustrated and lacking the words to express it. "I don't know what this is."

She blinked, *finally* showing an emotion that wasn't haughty disdain. Shock or something like it. Confusion, definitely. She *should* be confused. He was damn confused himself.

"What *what* is?"

"This…feeling. What I feel for you. I don't understand it. I can't say I like it. It's like…a disease."

"I'm a *disease*?"

"That isn't what I meant."

She inhaled carefully. "No, I suppose it isn't." Her eyebrows knitted together, and she studied him. It made his chest feel too tight, and it made him want to do things. Touch her, for one.

She was…she was so much better than him. He knew what he was. What he deserved. It sure as hell wasn't her.

"Reece…" She trailed off, but just his name sounded tortured. Like she was dealing with at least some of the tension he was. But that was stupid, because she was just worried about Henry. About her life.

"I suppose the difference between us," she said after a while, "is I know what I feel, but I can't trust it." She took a step toward him. Her fingertips touched his jaw, featherlight and with some trepidation, as if she might dart away at any second.

He held himself so still he wasn't even sure he was breathing.

Her eyes looked directly into his. "You're a good man," she said firmly. "Against my will, I can't help but trust you. It's myself I don't trust."

She seemed…sad about that, and her fingers didn't fall off his face. She didn't step away. She just…looked at him, like if she did it long enough, something would change.

Maybe he could change it. He could touch her back. He could kiss her. He could change *everything*. Hadn't he done that? Over and over again? Change his life in the face of circumstances that shouldn't have allowed him to change?

His hand settled on her waist with half a thought to draw her near, even as that insidious voice he'd tried to silence his whole life told him he didn't have the right. She didn't step away. She didn't drop her hand. She sucked in a breath, but she didn't turn away.

Without warning, there was the sound of a faint crash, then heavy footsteps, right before a large figure appeared at the end of the hall.

Reece felt like a guilty kid with a stolen piece of candy as he pulled his hand off Lianna's waist. He glanced at her and realized she'd gone stiff and pale as her hand dropped from his face.

"That's Holden Parker," he offered, understanding that the appearance of a stumbling, injured man wasn't exactly the norm for her. "Another operative." One who was sporting a bloody shirt and an unnaturally uneven gait. "Parker, did you get shot again?"

Holden flashed a grin as he stumbled past them and toward his room. "A mere flesh wound, friend."

Reece frowned. Holden looked pale, and there was way too much blood on his shirt. He also didn't stick around to introduce himself to Lianna, which wasn't like Holden at all.

"I think you should go see if he's okay," Lianna said, watching where Holden had gone. "That didn't look good."

"Right."

She returned her gaze to him and then smiled. "Good night, Reece," she said softly, before turning away and disappearing into the room where Henry was asleep.

Reece blew out a breath. He had no idea what any of that…meant. But he figured that was best. He hadn't done anything she'd regret, and he could…get a good night's sleep and shove it all down tomorrow. Focus on the task at hand. Keep her and Henry safe.

No matter the cost.

He strode into Holden's room without knocking. Holden was sitting on his bed, failing at stripping off his own shirt.

"Did you call Betty?" Reece demanded, already knowing the answer. Holden Parker was an explosives expert. He was impulsive and often got himself injured in the line of duty. He also *hated* doctors—not Betty specifically, but any medical attention whatsoever.

"I'm fine," he grumbled predictably.

"You were shot. What were you even doing?"

"Asking the wrong questions of the wrong people, apparently. Someone took offense to me asking questions about the guy who Sabrina tied up earlier. Then I took offense to them trying to 'escort' me elsewhere." Holden flashed a cocky grin. "You should see the other guy."

"You need Betty."

"I'll live. Yet again. Who's the lady?" Holden nodded toward the hallway and waggled his eyebrows.

"Don't worry about it," Reece muttered, knowing Holden was just being Holden and there was no need to get bent out of shape.

"Dibs. I understand."

Offended against his will, Reece shook his head. "There's no *dibs*. Have some respect. She's a *mother*."

"Moms like me," Holden said with a grin. "And I like them."

Reece pulled his phone out of his pocket, pressed Betty's name.

"Don't you—" Holden reached for the phone, but a hiss of pain had him stopping short.

"Bet? Holden's here."

"Did that moron get shot again?" she asked.

"He did. Looks bad. He couldn't even stop me from making the phone call."

Betty swore softly. "I'll get my stuff and be there in a few. Don't let him leave that room."

"Got it." Reece ended the call and shoved his phone back in his pocket again. "If you try to jump out the window, you're only going to earn yourself a trip to the actual hospital."

Holden sneered. "I hate you."

"Yeah, yeah."

Holden's gaze turned sharp and assessing. "Looks like I interrupted a tender moment."

Reece shrugged, refusing to give in to Holden's attempt to irritate him out of the room so he could evade Betty's impending arrival.

"She's the innkeeper, right? The one we're trying to protect."

"She is."

"Never seen you get involved in an assignment before."

Again, Reece shrugged.

"I tell you what. You couldn't pay me to get involved with someone during an assignment. Talk about a disaster waiting to happen."

"Good thing I'm not involved, then."

Holden snorted. "You're up to your eyeballs in involvement, Montgomery. I can't imagine anything worse. Screws with your judgment, your self-preservation instincts. Screws with *everything*."

"Thanks for the pep talk," Reece muttered. He heard the rattle of the medical cart. "Do I need to strap you down so Betty can look at you, or are you going to be a good boy?"

Holden laughed. "I bet I could outmaneuver you even with a gunshot wound."

Reece raised an eyebrow. "Want to try it?"

Betty sighed behind him. "Is there anything worse than fragile male egos?"

Reece moved out of the way so she could push her cart inside.

"I swear to God, Holden, if you fight me, I'm going to sedate you against your will."

There were more grumbles from Holden as Betty got to work. Reece left the room more bothered by the exchange than he'd like to admit.

Couldn't pay me to get involved with someone during an assignment. Talk about a disaster waiting to happen.

Yes, it was. It *was*. So he needed to get himself together. And fast.

Chapter Thirteen

Lianna woke up to Henry whispering her name in an urgent tone.

"I have to pee," he whispered, dancing around by the door. "But I don't know where to go."

Lianna was out of bed and to the door in a flash. She didn't even worry about the fact she was in pajamas as she ushered Henry out the door to the nearest restroom she'd been shown last night.

Henry swooped in and closed the door, clearly making it in the nick of time. Lianna let out a breath of relief. Which ended on an inelegant gasp she couldn't hide when she looked up to see Reece in the hallway, walking toward her.

He was wearing shorts and a sweatshirt, clearly having had some kind of workout, as there was a ring of sweat around his neck. His face was dripping, and he looked at her with a wariness she didn't fully understand.

Much like she didn't understand the shiver of attraction that ran through her when he was grimy and sweaty. It should be a turnoff, but she found herself thinking things she definitely, *majorly* shouldn't. Especially with her son just on the other side of this door.

"Morning," he offered.

"Good morning. Uh. How's your friend?"

"He'll be fine," Reece said gruffly. "He's always just fine."

The door shot open and Henry came out already talking a mile a minute. Lianna stopped him by shooting her arm out to stop his forward progress. "Wash your hands."

Henry groaned and threw his head back, making an epic drama over the short, barely satisfactory handwashing he then performed. Lianna winced at the way he got water *everywhere*.

"Can you play in the arcade with me today?" Henry asked Reece, practically jumping up and down.

Reece's grave expression softened into an affectionate smile. "I will a little bit later, buddy. I've got some meetings this morning. So does your mom."

"Does that mean I can play with Sabrina?" Henry asked hopefully.

"I think Betty is going to play with you this morning. I hope you're ready. She's a tough one to beat."

"I can do it!"

"What about breakfast?" Lianna asked.

"There's a little breakfast buffet of sorts set up in the kitchen. Feel free to help yourself once you're…" He trailed off, his eyes taking such a quick tour of her body she almost thought she'd imagined it. "Dressed."

Heat stole up Lianna's cheeks as she became expressly aware that she wasn't wearing a bra. She tried to *casually* cross her arms over her chest, but it was of no matter. Reece had his eyes on a door farther down the hall. "Take your time with breakfast," he was saying. "We'll meet in the conference room around nine."

Lianna didn't say anything to that. There was no point when he'd disappeared into a room and shut the door.

Henry had already bounded back into the room they were staying in. He was chattering about video games as Lianna handed him his clothes from yesterday to change into. He'd need a change of clothes. Little boys were too smelly to wear the same clothes two days in a row.

But that was a problem for later. She changed back into her own clothes from yesterday and tried to forget everything about Reece and focus on the task at hand. On what she had to do.

She had an idea, but she wasn't sure how to convince Shay and especially Reece it was a good one. A necessary one.

She wrangled Henry to breakfast and fought with him over how much he had to eat before he could play arcade games. It amazed her that even in these circumstances he could be such a...carefree boy.

Thank God for small favors.

At nine, Lianna left Henry in Betty's care and headed for the conference room, pulse beating too hard in her neck. Shay and Reece were already in the room, and Elsie was tapping away at her computer, giving Lianna the impression she hadn't left at all since last night. Sabrina and the man from

yesterday—what was his name? Holden, maybe—
were sitting at the table, conversing in low tones.

Everyone grew silent when she stepped into the
room. It made her feel even more out of place than
she already felt. Like she was to blame for all this,
when she knew she wasn't. Neither Todd's choices
nor this group entering her life were her fault at all.

But that didn't ease her discomfort at being the
center of attention.

Reece pulled a chair back from the table and gestured for her to sit. She tried to arrange her face into
a semblance of a smile as she took it.

They already had the game room up on the monitor, though the sound was off. Still, she could see
Henry dancing around a game while Betty's focus
was on the screen of the game.

"We have a variety of options here," Shay said,
bringing the meeting to order with an air of control
and leadership that impressed Lianna. Everyone's
attention was on Shay, and Lianna had little doubt
everyone in the room would follow her orders without question.

"None of them are set in stone. We're still in the
brainstorming phase, of course."

Lianna didn't have time for brainstorming. Not
when Henry needed home and school and…a life.
"They think I know something, and unfortunately,
me knowing Todd's real name probably only re-
inforced that belief."

"Yes, we agree. Which puts you in a lot of danger, especially since you *don't* know the informa-

tion they're looking for." Shay paused for a moment. "Right?"

Lianna nodded. "I've told you everything I know. Unless they're looking for his real name or two of the many groups he was involved with, I'm at a loss."

"And whatever group this guy was working for is…beyond secretive," Elsie said, gesturing at her screen though Lianna couldn't see it from her seat. "Even with the guy's real identity, I'm not digging much up on the group he works for."

"There's nothing your husband might have left you…a banking number, a deposit box key…anything really, that someone might be after?"

"No. I never went through Todd's things. I just tossed them. When Henry and I moved to Denver, I paid someone to get rid of whatever was left. I wanted a fresh start."

"Still, there could have been something in his belongings that connected to them. They could think you have it."

"Maybe, but… Obviously I don't know who came and asked me questions after the murder. Aside from the FBI. But there weren't questions like those. It was always people quizzing me on what I knew about his work."

Shay drummed her fingers on the table.

"This group had listening devices all over that inn. It's possible they never sent people to question her directly. If they're this concerned about secrecy, maybe they didn't want to risk even asking questions," Reece said, appearing much calmer and more detached than he had at any point yesterday.

Lianna envied him that control.

"If they got devices in the inn, who's to say they didn't have devices everywhere else she lived?" Sabrina suggested.

"But a year of listening to someone is a little over-the-top, even for this kind of a group," Holden pointed out. "They'd want to act. Why haven't they acted?"

Lianna closed her eyes. Her thoughts had been going in the same relentless circles for days. "This is the problem. We don't know. We don't have anything to go on. Which is why…" Nerves assaulted her, but she linked her fingers together and focused on the end result.

A safe, happy life for Henry.

"I have an idea. I'm sure you're all experts at… tactics and whatnot, but I'm an expert at, well, me."

Shay leaned back in her chair. Lianna didn't dare look at Reece. She knew she wouldn't be able to keep the aura of detached calm she so desperately wanted to portray.

"I want to go back to the inn. As soon as possible. No matter what, even if I knew his name, they think I'm stupid. They think they can win. Which means I have to play that role. Just like I did for the FBI and everyone else. The stupid, manipulated wife who didn't even know her husband was some dirty operative for who knows how many criminal groups."

"You aren't that, and you're not going back alone. That's suicide," Reece interrupted. With none of the calm he'd just been using.

"No, I don't want to go alone." Lianna blew out a

breath in an effort to settle her nerves. She turned to Reece's dark, furious gaze. "I want you to go with me."

REECE OPENED HIS mouth to tell her there was no way in hell she was going to do this, but then her words sank in.

She wanted him to go with her.

"You see, if I did it once, why not again?"

"Do what once?" Shay asked. Reece didn't like that look. Like she was considering this insanity.

"Fall for a guy. Let him manipulate me into being whatever front or disguise he needed. If I go back to the inn with Reece, and we play it up for the listening devices—that he's trying to get information out of me by pretending to be interested—they'll eat it up."

"They won't come near you knowing Reece is there," Holden said, but it wasn't as dismissive as Reece would have liked. It was more the way they often hashed out a plan.

"If it was only him? Why not?"

"They're patient. Clearly."

"Sure, but I imagine me knowing Todd's real name will speed things along. Especially if we act like I've told Reece something important."

Shay blew out a breath. "I have the utmost faith in my operatives, Lianna, but if they did send in a team to get you—it would be a team. And Reece couldn't fight off an entire team of bad guys, even if he wanted to."

"Depends on how many," Reece muttered. If it had been another assignment, he might have pushed that plan, but this was Lianna. How could he possibly take chances with Lianna?

"You've thought this through," Sabrina said thoughtfully. "You've got a ruse. You've got a well-trained guy to play it out with you. What about the kid?"

"I want him as far away from this as possible," Lianna said firmly. "At first I thought to have him go to my grandparents in Denver, but that would put my grandparents in danger, too, wouldn't it?"

Shay nodded. "Would your grandparents be willing to come here? Normally I'd set everyone up in a safe house, but until Elsie identifies this group, I don't want to take that kind of chance."

"I think they would. If I could speak to them first." Reece watched her shake away the glimmer of doubt. He wished he didn't understand so well that she thought her grandparents might hold her to the mistake she'd made with Todd, might think she was being taken in again.

Because she'd said as much last night. She could put her trust in him, but everything that had happened with her dead husband made it hard to trust herself.

Yet she was the best mother he'd ever seen. Strong in the face of what must have been a yearlong nightmare for her.

"So the plan would be to send you and Reece back to the inn. Playact for the mics that you know something. And wait for them to show up. Then what?"

"Sabrina and Holden can be nearby," Reece said, the plan taking shape in his mind. He still didn't *like* it. He'd rather Lianna and Henry stay carefully holed away for, well, forever. But he understood Lianna's desire to give Henry a real life. Back to school, back to the home he'd only just gotten accustomed to. They both deserved a real life free of Todd Kade and all he'd wrought. "Carefully placed, but near enough to close in once a detail shows up. Return ambush. We're the ones getting intel from them."

"It could work," Holden agreed with a nod.

"With that hole in your gut?" Sabrina asked with a smirk.

Holden only grinned at her. "I could take *you* down with a hole in the gut. Why not some secret group?"

"In your dreams."

"Children," Shay said mildly to Holden and Sabrina. She turned to Lianna specifically. "It's not without risks."

"I understand that," Lianna said. Her hands were clasped so tightly in her lap her knuckles were white, but she pressed on with an impressive outward calm. "I don't think there's a course of action here that doesn't have risks. There's one wrinkle. The listening devices. I imagine they know I know about them. I did take one off the smoke detector."

"Do a sweep and miss one," Elsie suggested, her eyes never leaving her computer. "Make it look like you just didn't know about it."

"That could work," Reece said thoughtfully. "The ones in the common areas were on the carbon monoxide detectors. If they can buy Lianna being dumb, I'm sure they can buy us being inept enough to only find the ones specifically on smoke detectors."

"Risky. They might read through that," Shay pointed out.

"Might. But I'm willing to bet they're going to underestimate until they have reason not to."

"Reece is right," Sabrina agreed. "Besides, if they do read through it, that doesn't change much. They know Lianna knows something. They know she's involved with some other group. To my way of thinking, the worst thing that happens is they *don't* come after her and we need a new plan."

Reece could think of a lot worse outcomes, but he kept those to himself. Because he'd do everything in his power to make sure none of them became an eventuality.

"So? We do it?" Lianna asked. She looked around the room, but clearly everyone was waiting for Shay to agree.

After a pause—dramatic, in Reece's estimation—Shay finally nodded. "We'll make the arrangements with your grandparents and work from there."

Chapter Fourteen

Lianna talked to her grandparents and parents on Shay's secure phone line that was supposed to be completely unable to be tapped on either end. Because apparently they were worried about her family being monitored.

Lianna tried not to let her fear thread through her voice as she spoke with them. As she explained the situation. As she silently *willed* them to believe her, not question her decision.

They had every right to be skeptical of her judgment after what she'd gone through with Todd. But they weren't. They asked questions, they expressed worry, but they didn't act like she was a fool for trusting these people.

"So we'll do a switch," Shay was saying, walking Lianna somewhere deeper in the house. Lianna didn't know where they were going, but she didn't ask. "Your grandfather is going to go shopping. One of our men will meet with him, switch clothes, and that way Henry will have a family member here, and your family will have an operative with them keeping a watch on things."

"How many operatives do you have?"

Shay smiled, opening a door and gesturing Lianna inside. "A variety. Full-time. Part-time. Not as many as we used to, but I have a lot of contacts. I know it's harder to trust someone you've never met, but Sabrina and Holden and Reece are the most experienced operatives I have, and I want them where the potential for danger is the highest."

Lianna tried to find some comfort in that, but she was sending a stranger to stay with her grandmother and parents. Who did that? Who—

Lianna's thoughts stopped short as she realized Shay had brought her into a bedroom. What must be Shay's own bedroom.

"I wanted some privacy. In other words, somewhere Reece wasn't going to come along and interrupt with his macho show of overprotection."

"Oh, he doesn't mean…"

"I know exactly what he means. Reece is a good guy. He cares about you, and before you start protesting that, too, it's obvious. The only person who's been here even close to as long as I have is Reece. I've seen more emotion out of the guy in the past week than I have in something like seven years." She paused before continuing. "A few years ago, our first leader was injured. A guy Reece really looked up to. I *know* it hit him hard, but I never *saw* it hit him hard. If you know what I mean."

"I don't…"

"He's a tough guy. They're *all* tough guys here. They're also good guys, which means sometimes they get all uppity about protecting the womenfolk, but it comes from a good place, an honest place. Even when that makes me want to punch them in the face, I get it."

Lianna was at a complete loss.

Shay glanced at her and seemed to read that. "My point is, Reece will do everything and anything to protect you. As he should, feelings or no. He's a trained soldier and operative, and you're not. That's how it works. That doesn't mean you shouldn't have the means to protect yourself, as well. Do you know how to shoot a gun?"

"Well, yes. My grandfather insisted I learn before I moved to the inn. He taught Henry the basics, too."

"That's good. Do you have a gun?"

"Yes. At the inn. I...keep it locked away and hidden. I don't really want Henry knowing it's there, but you know, safety in such an isolated area and..."

"That's fine for when Henry's there," Shay said dismissively. "But when it's just you and Reece, keep it on you. No matter what Reece says."

"You don't think he'll want me to carry a gun?"

"He's just going to think he can protect you on his own, and he's probably right. But this is about..."

Finally, Lianna was starting to understand what Shay was trying to get across. "It's about standing on your own two feet."

"Exactly. He's going to have a hard time understanding that. Not because he's a pigheaded man, but because he has a deep instinct to protect. He's conditioned to protect. It's what we do. But being a woman, I know that... It's not always the most effective mode of feeling safe. So you carry the gun around."

Shay rummaged around in a drawer and pulled out what looked like a sidearm holster. "Take this one. I assume you don't have anything like that."

"No. No, I don't."

"There. Now you can stay armed and dangerous."

"Thanks." Lianna didn't know quite what else to say. Or why they'd had to come into Shay's private quarters for this exchange. But Shay didn't make a move to usher Lianna back out, which meant there was…more to this.

"Look, I know it's a lot. To trust us. To put your life and your family in our hands."

"I don't really have another choice."

"I guess not. Listen… It isn't my job to tell you what to do. But it kind of comes with the territory. Being able to analyze people and if they're ready to take on a challenge… I have to be able to do that. For my operatives."

"Reece seems ready to handle any challenge."

"Yes, he is. Even as…invested as he is in this, I think he's capable and ready. I meant you, Lianna."

Lianna let out a laugh, hoping it didn't sound as bitter as it felt. "Another choice I don't have. Ready or not, here it comes."

"Yes and no. You could work on trusting yourself. One of the best ways a woman can be safe, stay safe, is to trust her gut. Listen to it. The gut doesn't lie."

That was never going to happen. Not after all the mistakes she'd made. "My gut lied. I never once thought Todd was…well, what he was."

"I'm going to have to disagree with you."

Lianna's mind whirled around that. This tough woman, who ran some *group* with operatives and men like Reece and Holden looking to her for approval, seemed to think Lianna's instincts were good. "You don't even know me."

"Sure, but you knew that Todd wasn't a good father, right? You told us he traveled to stay away. Your gut knew that wasn't right. Sure, you couldn't have fathomed he was some kind of two-faced, lying bastard, but you *knew* something wasn't right."

Lianna felt like crying, because that wasn't any better. Knowing and doing what she'd done. "I stayed," she said around the lump in her throat, fingering the holster Shay had given her.

"Women have stayed with worse for much smaller reasons. No one goes through life without getting fooled once or twice. No one gets through life without regrets born of…well, all sorts of things. It's kind of part and parcel of being human."

"I find it hard to believe you've been taken in and fooled by a man. Especially a man that was the father of your child."

"No, not the father of my child. But I have my own mistakes and regrets, ones I had to forgive myself for. It took a long time, but I got a lot more accomplished, helped myself and other people a lot better, once I did."

Lianna looked up at her and saw…well, those regrets Shay had spoken of, right there in her expression as she continued to speak.

"We all make mistakes when love is involved.

Fathers to your kids. Siblings. Parents. Friends. We all get mixed up and let feelings override reason, or make us ignore our gut feelings. Doesn't mean your gut lies."

"How can you tell the difference?"

"I think knowing there *is* a difference is the first step."

Lianna didn't know how that could be true, but she trusted this woman. Believed this woman. How could she not?

REECE WAS PRETTY sure Henry could spend the next year in the arcade room and only come up for food and bathroom breaks. Maybe a little sleep. Personally, Reece would like to get the kid outside, but he didn't have any say. Not to mention, Henry probably deserved to do whatever he wanted for the time being.

"How long are we going to have to stay here?" Henry asked. His gaze was still on the screen, that glazed-over look to his eyes, but the way he stood had changed. As if he was a little bit more alert of his surroundings.

"It depends, but I have it on good authority your great-grandpa is going to come here to stay with you."

Henry didn't stop his game, but his gaze went sharp and his eyebrows drew together. "Why?"

"Why not?"

"Well, we're in some danger, right? I don't want Gramps to be in danger."

"You and your great-grandfather will be safe here. I promise."

Henry's game character died on the screen. He turned to Reece, expression…very close to unreadable, especially for a seven-year-old.

"Why is he coming here? Really?"

Reece figured Lianna should be the one to tell him, but he could hardly lie to the kid. "Your mom and I are going to…" How the hell did he explain what they were going to do? "We're going to try to get some answers on what's going on."

"You're going to go away?"

"Not away, exactly. We're going to go look into some things. We want you and your mom to be able to go home and be safe. So we're going to make sure we can arrange that." Could he possibly be any more vague or any less reassuring?

"My dad used to go away a lot."

There was an accusation in that sentence. Blame. Reece felt an unaccustomed stab of…hurt. Guilt he would have understood, but how could he be hurt by a young boy's words?

"This isn't like that," Reece said as reassuringly as he could manage. He crouched down so he could be eye to eye with Henry. He put his hand on the boy's shoulder. "It's my job to keep you and your mom safe. Sometimes we have to go away to figure out how to do that, but that doesn't mean we won't come back. It doesn't mean that our goal isn't…going home. Both of you going home and being safe."

"What about you?"

"What about me?"

"Where's your home? You said you didn't live here. Where will you go home and be safe?"

Reece had been shot, been in a building when it exploded. He'd been stabbed. He'd been neglected by his own parents. He wasn't sure anything had ever hurt quite as deeply as that simple question did.

"This building might not be my home, but this group? It's my home. It's what I do."

Henry chewed on his bottom lip. "You're going to keep the bad men away from Mom, right?"

Reece studied Henry. There was something about the boy... A guardedness Reece hadn't seen in him before. "Can you tell me what you know about the bad men?"

Henry shrugged. "It's just... You'll protect her. You'll make sure nothing happens to her."

Reece knew Henry was worried. Scared. Whether he'd had a good father or not, the man had been murdered. It was only natural Henry should have some lingering fears about losing other people in such a sudden, violent manner.

But there was something about those questions, and the direct, imploring blue gaze of the boy.

"I will," Reece agreed, vowed. But he didn't stand up or let go of Henry's shoulder. "Is there something you want to tell me? Something you're worried about?"

Henry was silent and still for longer than Reece had ever noticed.

A ripple of dread skittered down his spine, but he didn't know what to do with it. Because Henry shook his head. Nothing he was worried about. Nothing he wanted to tell.

He'd been through a hard time. Reece was reaching to be reading into his reactions and legitimate fears like this. But long after he'd left Henry under Sabrina's watchful eye, the interaction bothered him.

He packed up what he thought he would need. Packed far more weapons than he'd originally gone in with. It would just be him and Lianna, so he didn't have to worry about the safety of having weapons around a young boy. All he had to worry about was keeping Lianna safe.

It's just... You'll protect her. You'll make sure nothing happens to her. Henry's words, and the careful, almost adult delivery of them, repeated in Reece's head the entire time. All the way up to when he went to seek out Lianna so they could head out.

She was in the kitchen with Henry and an older gentleman. She was smiling at both of them, and even with the worry around her eyes, the *love* in her eyes for the two men around her cut straight through him.

More than want. More than…anything he'd ever known. He thought of last night and the way she'd touched him and he—

Had to focus on keeping her safe. That was the only thing.

"Reece," she said, finally noticing him. She stood and Reece noted she hadn't touched her plate of food. "This is my grandfather. Hank Young. Grandpa, this is Reece Montgomery."

The older gentleman stood and extended a hand.

His handshake was firm and his eyes were stern, but his greeting was kind enough. "Good to meet you. I hear you've been keeping our kids safe."

"Yes, sir. I plan to keep it that way."

"Good, good. We're all eager for this to be over."

Lianna walked over to Henry and pulled him into a hug. "Be good for Grandpa Hank and everyone here. I'll be back soon. I promise." She kissed his head, smoothed his hair. Reece watched as she took a deep breath and had to *force* herself to leave her son's side.

That feeling from earlier swelled up in him, threatening to take him completely under.

She walked over to her grandfather, gave him a hug and whispered something in his ear. But Reece hardly had time to recover before Henry bounded out of his chair.

"Bye, Reece," Henry said, flinging his arms around Reece's legs. He squeezed tight and it seemed to squeeze around Reece's heart like a vise.

"See ya soon, kid. No worries, okay?"

Henry let him go and nodded, but there were fears in the boy's eyes. Fears he didn't voice. Reece couldn't help but frown over that as he led Lianna into the hallway.

"Does Henry know something?" he asked quietly, leading her to the front door.

She inhaled, and he knew she was trying to keep her composure over leaving Henry behind. "He's just so smart," Lianna said, somehow sounding proud and sad at the same time. "I'm sure he's overheard things I'd rather he didn't. I'm sure he's put together things I'd rather he didn't."

Reece nodded. That had to be it. Regardless, they had other things to concern themselves with. "Are you ready for this?"

Lianna lifted her chin, a stubborn fighter's light in her eye. "I am."

Chapter Fifteen

The sun was setting as Reece drove her up the familiar drive to her inn. The kind of early-summer sunset that usually gave her a giddy hopefulness that if the world could be *that* beautiful, things couldn't be *that* bad.

Of course, things were pretty bad right now, so it was hard to access her usual joy.

"We're going to do a quick sweep of the area," Reece said, pulling to a stop. "Then the entire building." He sounded every inch the...whatever he was. *Operative.*

"We'll want to check your car, too," he added.

"My car?"

"We're just covering all our bases." She supposed he thought his voice was reassuring, but the way his eyes seemed to take in everything around them didn't put her at any kind of ease.

Still, she appreciated that he said *we*. It somehow made her feel...part of it. Even when she was reeling from the idea of a *sweep* of the area.

"If they can set up listening devices, they could easily set up cameras. So we're going to have to make it look like we're looking, but not too closely. If they're watching, we want to give the impression that we're cautious, but at least a little inept."

"That we're…" Lianna trailed off, irritated that heat was creeping up her cheeks. "I mean, I think we need to make it look like we're…"

"We're?"

He wasn't going to make this easy on her, and that irritated her enough she straightened in her seat. *"Involved,"* she said icily. "Women do stupid things for men all the time. And vice versa."

He made a noise, not quite an affirmation but not an argument, either. But he got out of the car, so she did, too. He grabbed the duffel he'd packed earlier. Lianna hadn't had anything to pack except the holster Shay had given her.

The evening was almost warm, and everything smelled and felt like summer. The green earth beneath her feet, the colorful pop of color from her gardens.

Lianna wished Henry were here. Wished this had all been a dream. She looked at the man standing in front of his car, waiting for her to close her door and walk to him. Maybe she didn't wish it was all a dream. Well, it was a stupid wish anyway, because this was her life.

He looked at her, and there was something like… confusion in his expression. Like he was at a loss over what to do. It dawned on her that he must not know *how* to look involved.

Now, surely a man like Reece had been involved with a woman before. She remembered how desperate and bewildered he'd been by his own feelings. She understood both those, but he'd never had… She didn't think he'd ever had anyone truly *care* for him, to the point he didn't even know how to fake it.

Unaccountably sad, she skirted the car and slid her hand into his, forcing a smile that didn't show all the sympathy inside of her. His hand was rough and warm, and even though she was talking about *pretending* to be involved, her heart skipped a beat like it didn't know the difference.

"I've still got your keys," Reece said, and she thought he was trying to be cheerful, but there was a rasp to his voice that didn't pull it off.

"Let's take a walk around the gardens first," Lianna said, hoping her forced attempt at cheer didn't sound deranged. "It looks like it rained, but I want to make sure nothing needs to be watered."

"Good one," he said under his breath.

Lianna doubted there would be any listening devices out here, but she felt like they couldn't take any chances for the moment. She'd play a role. She'd learned how to get rather good at that, she thought.

So Reece dumped his duffel on the porch and they walked around the house. Lianna went ahead and checked the soil in her pots and beds, determining nothing needed to be watered. She chattered on about the flowers since she didn't know what else to do, and Reece nodded along as though he was listening.

It felt cozy and intimate and *right*, and Lianna wondered what the hell was wrong with her that she could enjoy something fake, knowing it wasn't real. Knowing she was in danger and her son was locked away with her grandfather just so he wasn't in the cross fire.

Once they'd done a full turn around the house, Reece released her hand. It felt like a loss, and she shivered.

"It's getting a little cold," Reece murmured. "Let's go inside. I didn't see anything that would be a camera or a listening device. I think the outside is clear."

Lianna nodded and they walked up the stairs of the porch. Reece grabbed his bag, then took her keys out of his pocket. He made a move as if he was going to hand them to her, then thought better of it.

He propped open the storm door and shoved the key in the main door's lock. "I have to look like I'm taking advantage of you," he said very, very quietly. "Using you. So I'm going to have to be a little heavy-handed. At least when there's a chance of being watched or listened to."

Lianna nodded silently, because she didn't know what else to do. He unlocked the door and stepped inside, flipping on the lights. Lianna followed. It smelled like home, and she relaxed even knowing someone could have been in here poking around, setting up cameras or more listening devices.

"Nice to be here without your kid, huh?" Reece said, his voice light and flippant and not Reece at all.

Lianna rubbed at the pain in her chest. He was lying, acting. She knew that. Still, she couldn't work it up to agree.

"Why don't you make us some dinner? I've got to go check on some things."

Lianna found this *version* of Reece made her

tongue-tied. She didn't know how to get used to him pretending to be someone else. Which gave her the uncomfortable realization that even when he'd lied to her in the beginning, he'd been himself. Maybe he hadn't been out taking nature photographs, but the stories he'd told, the way he'd *been*, was just…him.

"Knock knock," Reece said sharply. "Anyone home? Some of us are hungry."

"Right. Right." She shook her head, trying to get it through her head he was playing a part, and she had to, as well. "Dinner. Let me see what I can whip up."

They parted ways and Lianna moved toward the kitchen. It was home, but she felt so out of sorts now it felt a bit like a stranger's house. Especially without Henry underfoot.

Still, the act of making dinner soothed and settled her. She couldn't fully relax without Henry here or when she knew anyone could be watching or listening and just waiting to strike, but she had a good talk with herself. She had to play her role. Stay in character. Not get flustered when Reece was so utterly un-Reece-like.

She'd finished the quick spaghetti dinner and was setting plates out on the dining room table when Reece finally returned.

"Found a few more of those listening devices in the rooms. Took care of the one you found and the rest."

"I don't know why they'd be listening in to guest rooms," Lianna said, trying to sound a mix of baffled and afraid. "I could lose this place if someone thought I did it."

"This is why it's important you tell me everything you know, Lianna. Who knows what you said without thinking while they were listening."

"I'm sure I've told you everything I remember."

Reece made a disbelieving sound, then prowled around the dining room. He'd said there was one in here, but as he came to take a seat at the table, he shrugged. "Don't see any in here."

"Do you think they'll come after me if you took care of the other listening devices?" She tried to sound scared. A little over-the-top scared. Someone who wouldn't even try to stand on her own two feet.

Then she wasn't standing on her own two feet. In a deft move, Reece had tugged her into his lap. She couldn't bite back the surprised squeak, especially when Reece's mouth moved to her ear.

She could feel the movement of his lips, the warmth of his breath, as he whispered into her ear. "No cameras anywhere. Only the listening devices that were there before. No one came back while we were gone, but with that big window there and the lights on in here, we can't be sure no one is watching."

Lianna tried to *relax*, to act. The idea that someone might be watching through the window was beyond disturbing, but what really bothered her was that her mind wasn't on that alone. It was on the fact she was *sitting* on Reece's lap. She could feel his body heat underneath her, the tension in his thighs under hers. The thing that shuddered through her was not close enough to fear as it should be.

He eased her off effortlessly and gently, and she

had to be about fifty different shades of red. But he went about eating the spaghetti as though this were all *normal*. Because he was good at this. At acting and being someone else.

Which she didn't understand, because he hadn't done that in the beginning. He hadn't put on *this* act with her. The only thing he'd pretended, as far as she could tell, was the nature photography.

But tonight he chatted and ate as if he was, well, Todd Part II. She should have been weirded out, but instead she was almost…relieved. If he could *pretend* to be someone like Todd…didn't that mean he really hadn't been pretending up until now?

They finished dinner and Reece made some condescending remark about letting her handle cleanup. He disappeared again and she tackled the dinner dishes. There was only one window in the kitchen and it was over the sink, but it only had a half blind. Someone could be out there watching her. Someone could…

She closed her eyes and took a deep breath. Reece wouldn't have left her alone if she was in immediate danger. Even for all his acting tonight, she knew that. Believed that.

Trust your gut. She was definitely out of practice when it came to that, but Reece was making it easier. Shay and the whole group of people working to help her made it easier. She didn't even know what to call their group, but she trusted them. With her son. With her grandfather. Basically, her life.

Doubts crept in, because she'd trusted wrongly before, but she just kept repeating Shay's advice.

Trust your gut. Her gut knew, despite the doubts, she was doing the only thing she could think to do. If it didn't work…

Well, she'd cross that bridge when she came to it.

She went through her normal routine, double-checking doors. She stayed as far away from the windows as she could, and she felt way more tense than usual. Also, there wasn't a baby monitor attached to her hip, none of Henry's snores making the house seem less isolated.

At another time, she might have enjoyed the quiet and the solitude. A vacation of sorts. But with danger lurking, the last thing she wanted to do was be separated from her son.

This is the best thing you can do to keep him safe.

She had to believe that. Had to.

Reece had left the door to the hallway on her side unlocked and open. Lianna had half expected him to disappear to his old attic room, but that didn't make sense, did it? Not that much about this did.

She moved to her room, the tension that already held her muscles tight and her breathing shallow not dissipating any. Because now what?

Her room door was open and Reece was sitting at her desk, tapping away on a laptop she didn't recognize. It was strange to see him here in her room. This had always been *her* room. A girl's space and then a woman's. Even Henry didn't care to spend much time here.

But there was a very large man at her desk who somehow didn't look as out of place as he should.

"Sorry to invade your space," he said, standing

up, and though the move was completely smooth and very *operative*-like, there was a sense that he was... uncomfortable. *Awkward.* Because here they didn't have to worry about listening devices anymore, so he was just...Reece. Normal Reece.

"I don't want you sleeping alone."

WELL, *THAT* HAD come out all wrong. Or maybe there was no right way to say it when he could still feel the way she'd settled into his lap. Warm, perfect curves, that scent of citrus about her. The way her cheeks kept flushing an irresistible shade of pink.

"Sorry. That's not what I..." He cleared his throat. It hadn't been easy to pretend to be some self-absorbed moron out there, knowing people could be watching, but it was harder to pretend everything away when it was just...them. No listening devices. Curtains closed. Here he could be himself, and he could be honest.

And you have to keep her safe.

Safe didn't always equal honesty, but she was here. She hadn't let him handle this...though that still irritated him. But her plan was good and he'd keep her safe.

"The thing is, they didn't break in while we were gone," Reece said. He didn't believe honesty was the best policy here, but apparently the truth was coming out anyway. "They didn't set up cameras or listening devices when no one was here, and they could have. They aren't waiting around for information."

Understanding dawned on her face and the way she went a little pale. "They just want me."

"That's my theory. Now, you don't have to worry tonight. Elsie patched into your cameras—outside and in the hallway there. Someone will be watching around the clock, but I think we should stick close. Like same-room close."

Lianna nodded.

"Lucky for us both, I can sleep almost anywhere, so the floor will be fine," he said, trying to sound... casual. About sleeping in the same room. Which was casual and about the mission.

Lianna blinked and looked at her bed. It was perfectly made, as she'd no doubt left it. Color rose in her cheeks again, but she turned away from him.

Reece took the opportunity to finish the video call he'd been making on the laptop.

"It's so weird being here without Henry," Lianna said, unnecessarily plumping a pillow on the bed.

"Hi, Mom."

She whirled around at the sound of Henry's voice. Eyes filling a little when she saw Henry on the screen. "Hi, baby." Without another thought, she was standing next to Reece, bent over so she could be close to the screen.

Reece nudged her into the chair and settled himself against the desk as Henry babbled happily.

"We had pizza for dinner. Then ice cream sundaes for dessert. Gramps read me the dumbest joke book. Hi, Reece! When are you guys coming back?"

Reece slid a look at Lianna. She smiled brightly and spoke calmly to Henry, assuring him they'd all be back together soon. Yet he could see that under the desk, she was twisting her fingers together, worrying.

There was no way to take the worry away, especially after they'd finished the call with Henry and spoken to Shay and Elsie, finding out there was absolutely no new information.

She still had a placid look on her face when the call ended, but her hands betrayed her, so he put his over hers. "When the mission is more frustrating than you want it to be, you just take it one step at a time. So next step? A good night's sleep."

"That sounds very practical," she said, and he knew she was trying to sound accepting rather than scathing, but she didn't quite make it.

Why did that make him smile?

But she looked down at his hands on hers, and her expression changed. Which he didn't have time to dwell on because she turned her hands in his so they were palm to palm, and that…short-circuited his brain.

He couldn't have said why. It was a simple touch, friendly at best, but… Well, when had he ever had much of that in his life? *Any* of that in his life?

"Why weren't you like that out there in the beginning?" she asked, and her gaze rose from their hands—still joined—to his eyes. She studied him, blue eyes dark and assessing. As if she could see through him. Understand him. In all the ways he didn't.

"Like what?" he asked through a too-tight throat.

"Pushy. Overconfident. It would have made sense."

"No. It wouldn't have."

"I was fooled by one man. I'm sure—"

"You're thinking like someone who goes off

one set of facts and makes all their decisions. I'm a trained operative. My job isn't just to go off the information I have. It's to observe and assess. This place was so neat and tidy. Cozy and like a home. The perfect kind you see on TV. Then there you were, and you...you were so competent."

She wrinkled her nose as if that was an insult rather than the compliment he meant it to be.

"When I asked why your name wasn't Young like the history of this house, you gave me this look and demanded to know if I had a personal question to ask about that. You didn't strike me as the type of woman who would be pushed around."

"And yet..."

"No 'and yet.' You're not. Maybe you made a mistake in trusting Todd Kade, but here you are. Fighting back. For your son. For yourself. Don't pretend like one mistake makes you someone you aren't."

She inhaled sharply, then let the breath go. Her hands squeezed his and she got to her feet. But she didn't move away, or take her hands out of his grasp. She stood there, right in front of him, holding his hands. "I'm starting to think you might be good for me, Reece Montgomery."

"Last night you said you couldn't trust yourself," he reminded her, because this felt like...dangerous ground. Lianna's hands in his. Some unknown battle light in her eyes.

She nodded, a little sadly. "I'm still working on that. It's strange but something about...well, you and your group. You trusted my plan. You're here, and I know you would have preferred to handle it alone.

But you all trusted me, and it made it easier to trust you. The easier *that* is, the more I seem to realize... I can trust myself. Or at least try to."

She moved closer, or leaned closer. Somehow she was *closer* and there was a buzzing in his head he didn't know how to stop. Everything inside of him was focused on her. This moment. The mission disappeared. Everything disappeared except *her*.

"Last night *you* said you don't know what this is," she said, her voice barely more than a whisper.

He couldn't pretend not to know what she meant. "I don't. I..."

"It's only because you never had it. No one ever gave you a reason to have it. A lot of people failed you when you were most vulnerable."

Uncomfortable with that word, with her sympathy that he felt drifted a little too close to pity, he shrugged. "I survived." He pulled his hands from hers, but she only reached up and placed a palm to his cheek.

"But survival doesn't give you a chance to care or be cared for." She moved closer, angling her mouth toward his. There was still a wariness there. Doubts, maybe. But her hand was on his face and his heart beat so hard in his chest it felt like a war was raging inside his rib cage. One that would leave him bloody and broken.

He'd never been able to avoid the real kind of war. Why would he be able to avoid this?

"I'm not sure danger and secrets is a great reason for caring about someone, but—"

"You're the only reason." Which seemed to destroy all the reason he'd been clinging to. All the sense. All his control. He closed the distance between them, pulling her against his chest.

And took all the things he didn't understand.

Chapter Sixteen

Reece kissed her like a starving man, and Lianna felt that she was perfectly amenable to being consumed by *this*. His arms banded around her so that it would have taken some serious work to escape.

She didn't want to escape. She wanted to give in to something.

You did this once before and look how that turned out.

But that little voice in her head wasn't as loud as it used to be, and Reece's hands smoothing over her back, molding her to the hard lines of his body, seemed to eradicate it completely.

At worst, mistakes had to be repeated to learn a lesson. Or so she told herself, because nothing about opening herself up to Reece felt like a mistake.

The kiss spun out, deep and consuming, his heart pounding as hard against her hand on his chest as hers was pounding inside her own.

The hands on her back pulled the hem of her shirt up, slowly revealing skin to the heated air around them. It wasn't cold, and still she shivered as she lifted her arms and let him pull the shirt over her head.

His eyes were dark and intense, but there was vulnerability under all that fierceness. He didn't understand it, and he'd probably never admit to being *vulnerable*. But she saw it. Wanted to protect it.

She could be good for Reece, just like he'd been good for her. She slid her hands under his T-shirt, pushing it up and out of the way until he discarded it like he'd discarded hers.

He was pure muscle, scarred skin. She ran her hands over the scars, stomach cramping at the things he must have seen. Endured.

There was a flicker of something on his face. Not embarrassment, but maybe discomfort. Or fear. So she leaned forward and pressed her mouth to one of his scars, to prove they only made him more beautiful. More...*him*.

Then she stretched up on her toes and pressed her mouth to his, wrapping her arms around his neck. She wanted to pour all the confusing, exhilarating emotion inside of her into him. Fill him with it. Until he understood, somehow, something she couldn't have articulated in words.

The kiss went wild, bigger and brighter than she'd ever known. They tugged at each other's pants, undressing the rest of the way, outside world and danger forgotten. He laid her on the bed and still there was such *control* in him, leashing back a desperation she could see in his eyes, feel in his kiss. He didn't seem to know how to let out. So she'd have to show him.

His body covered her like it had been made to. He touched her like he'd known how for years. Every kiss took her deeper and deeper into something she wasn't sure *she* understood. So she held on for dear life. As pleasure ebbed into pleasure, wave crashed into wave, and hope bloomed as pure and simple as if she'd never been hurt, she didn't want to think. She didn't want to worry. For this brief moment in time, she wanted to feel and savor and *enjoy*.

It was a joy, to be with someone like this. To be with *Reece* like this. To feel him inside of her, to hold him as he joined her over that edge of bliss.

They stayed there, tangled together, until she dozed off, spent and exhausted and…happy.

When she woke up with the morning sunlight streaming on her face, Reece wasn't in bed with her. She knew he'd slept there for a while because she'd woken up once in the dark and nuzzled closer to him. His arm had come around her, holding her tight.

But now he was up and dressed, bustling around the room. It was…almost as nice as waking up to him. Him moving about, doing things, as if he belonged here. She found she wanted him to belong here even knowing she had no idea how that would work.

Maybe you could have discussed that before… Lianna blinked at the sudden realization. This wasn't so simple as wanting to take care of someone who'd never had that. It wasn't as simple as liking him. This deep, tangled and inconvenient giving in to something she hadn't planned was…something more. Was it love?

No. No, she wasn't being this stupid again. She'd thought she'd fallen in love with Todd at first sight. A week wasn't much better. Especially a week where she'd been threatened. That meant she wasn't thinking clearly.

But she didn't feel muddled. She didn't find that she was talking herself into things like she had with Todd—so desperate for a love that didn't come with the strings of family.

She sat up in bed, frustrated with her own feelings. She didn't have to figure out everything right this second. Yes, they'd slept together, and it had been…wonderful. That didn't mean she needed to immediately know exactly what she felt and exactly what they were going to do about it.

Reece looked up, seeming unsurprised she was awake. "We'll want to drop some hints this morning," he said briskly. "That you know something you aren't telling me. Over breakfast, I'm thinking. You'll say something along the lines of wanting to open the inn, wanting Henry to come home, and I'll be dismissive. We can spend the rest of the morning away from the listening devices. Come back at lunch and I'll escalate the pressure. Bit by bit. We'll give it a day or two, and if they still don't act, I'll really explode. If you have to make something up, we'll figure it out beforehand."

She didn't know what to say to all that. He had plans. He was ready to face the day. She was…naked. She held the sheet up to her chest and tried to follow… any of what he'd said.

Breakfast. Pretending she knew something. Trying to draw someone out to…what? Demand information from her? Try to kidnap her?

This was your idea, remember?

She swallowed. This was the plan, the focus. Last night was the...well, distraction. She had to change gears as quickly as he had.

But when she looked at him again, he was standing at the end of the bed just *staring* at her. She might have felt self-conscious, naked with only a sheet held up to her chest, but she recognized that stare. It was the same look he'd given her in the hallway when he'd said he didn't know what this was. There was just *so much* inside this man that he didn't know how to let out, and she found that her doubts paled in the face of that.

She wanted to help him. She wanted...everything.

"I don't know how to do this," he said, as if each word was dragged across shattered glass.

Lianna felt her own throat tighten up. It felt too close to a goodbye, and she didn't want... Would he walk away because he didn't understand? Because it was too much for him? Would *she*? When she had a son to think of far above her own feelings.

"But I want to," he said, and she wouldn't say his words were *certain* so much as a simple truth he didn't know what to do with.

She swallowed at the lump in her throat. "Well, I guess we have to figure out how to do it, then."

Silence stretched between them and too much distance. She wanted to go to him, but...

He frowned and looked at the door. She would have dismissed the sound herself, but his acknowledgment of it made her realize what it had been. The faint sound of a car door being shut.

"Stay put," he ordered, and was out of her bedroom before she could argue.

She scowled at the space where he'd been. No, she would not stay put. She eyed the holster Shay had given her. She would stand on her own two feet. Love and future or not.

THE CAR THAT was parked next to his was sleek, dark and expensive. The man who stood next to it was much the same. Reece didn't know what to think.

On the one hand, whoever was after Lianna and what she knew wasn't just going to roll up in plain view and walk in…alone.

On the other hand, Lianna didn't have any reservations, her website said the Bluebird was temporarily closed, and nothing about this man and his appearance felt *right*.

He heard Lianna enter the living room, where he was watching the man's approach. He frowned. "I told you to stay put." Maybe he'd said that more because he wasn't sure how to find his normal control when she was near.

Last night had been… He couldn't categorize it as a mistake. Not when it felt as right as anything ever had. Not when she seemed to know who he was and what he needed when he wasn't sure *he* did. But he should have been focused on the *assignment*. Not his feelings.

The look she gave him seemed to say, *I'm not going to follow all your orders*, but she didn't say anything. Hopefully because she remembered they'd left a listening device in the kitchen.

She stood next to him, peering out the window.

She leaned forward and squinted at the man. "Dr. Winston," she said, mild surprise in her tone but no sense of alarm.

"Who?"

"My…doctor." She straightened her clothes unnecessarily. "Therapist, that is. From Denver. After Todd…"

She was trying not to seem embarrassed, but he could see the discomfort in her gaze, in the slight pink of her cheeks. "Understandable," he said, cutting off her explanations. Because after what she'd been through, it *was*, and as someone who'd had to undergo his fair share of mental health evaluations either through foster care or the military, he was hardly going to let her be embarrassed over it.

Of course, that wasn't really the image he was trying to portray for whoever was listening. He had to stop thinking about…everything else and focus on the fake persona he was supposed to be. "But what's he doing here?"

"I couldn't say. I haven't spoken to him since I left Denver. He wasn't very supportive of the move. Didn't think I was ready, mentally." She didn't meet Reece's gaze as she spoke quickly. "But look, he's got a bag. I guess maybe he thought he'd…come stay."

"A little blurring of professional lines, don't you think?"

She finally looked at him, expression a little haughty. "I don't know *what* to think, Reece."

"Let me handle him."

She huffed in indignation. "Why on earth would I do that?" She closed her eyes and winced, clearly forgetting herself for a second. Well, at least he wasn't the only one. When she spoke next, it was softer. More pleading.

"I know him, Reece. He's a trained, certified therapist who has nothing to do with this."

"That you know of."

Her mouth dropped open and her eyes went wide, not an act. "Are you suggesting my *therapist* was in on this?"

"Maybe not from the beginning, but anyone watching you could have paid enough attention. Could have considered you might tell your therapist something. This is all about information, as far as we know. Your therapist would be a natural target."

She paled, and he felt like a plodding jerk. Surely there was a better way to tell her that. A better way to do…all of this. He blew out a breath and tried to find it, but she was collecting herself. The way she always did.

"You're right," she said, and though her voice wavered, she was back in control. "You don't think he's in danger, do you? Should we—"

"We should see what the man wants, and once he's gone, you'll tell me everything you ever told him." He tried to sound stern for the listeners.

"Of course, Reece," she said in a conciliatory way that scraped against his nerves. It was an act, but that didn't mean parts of it didn't grate.

A knock sounded on the front door and Reece went to it and answered it, with Lianna at his heels. She quickly swept past him, though, and smiled at the doctor, holding the screen door open so he could step inside.

"Dr. Winston. This is a surprise."

"Hello, Lianna. Not a bad one, I hope."

Reece hated the man. Immediately. If sight had made him suspicious, the way the man spoke and looked at Lianna made him downright territorial.

Lucky for him, he was playing the role of a man who'd be *very* territorial. And kind of a jerk.

"What's all this, Lianna?"

"Oh." She blinked, and Reece could see clearly she had to remind herself that he was playing a role, but it worked. To someone who didn't know the situation, it would seem like she was what she was going to pretend to be. A woman too involved with an overbearing man. "Reece. This is… Um."

"Reece Conrad," Reece said, sliding past Lianna and holding out a hand.

The doctor looked at it and didn't seem at all surprised to see a man here. Or the inn being closed.

Strike two.

Finally, he shook Reece's hand and Reece made a show out of squeezing too hard. The doctor's expression hardened, so Reece smiled broadly.

He'd forgotten how enjoyable playing a role could be.

"I'm Dr. Winston," the man said. "And you are?"

"Oh, I'm a friend of Lianna's." He stepped back, slung his arm around Lianna's shoulders and gave them a squeeze. "Didn't know we were going to have company. Thought you closed the reservations for the week, hon."

"Oh, I did," Lianna assured him, sounding nervous, like she was afraid of displeasing him. *That* he didn't like so much, but at least he knew it was an act. She slid her arm around his waist as if trying to reassure him.

"My wife and I were on vacation, going up to Devil's Tower and the like. We were so close I just thought I'd stop in and see how Lianna was doing." He smiled. It struck Reece as a cold, calculated smile.

Strike three.

"You could have called," Reece said, not even trying to be polite.

"I suppose I should have."

"No, don't be silly," Lianna said, looking up at him imploringly. "Reece, Dr. Winston was such a help to me before I moved here."

"What kind of help?"

"Oh. Well…" Lianna looked down at the floor and never finished her sentence, looking perfectly embarrassed.

"Perhaps I could talk to Lianna alone? Doctor to patient? There are confidentiality rules, of course, and I'd like to discuss previous treatment."

Sure you do, buddy. "I don't think—"

"You did say you were going to check on that loose porch railing for me, didn't you? You could do that while Dr. Winston and I have a quick chat, and then I'm sure he'll be on his way, won't you?" She turned a tremulous smile on Dr. Winston.

"Of course."

Reece was loath to leave Lianna alone with this smooth operator, but the hint to go outside was a good one. He could look through the good doctor's car and see what he found, all while keeping a decent enough eye on Lianna. And having Elsie run the man, of course.

Lianna smiled up at him and gave him a gentle nudge out the door. She had her hip to him and patted it surreptitiously.

Underneath the fabric of her T-shirt was a lump of something. She had a gun on her. Well, that was some comfort, he supposed. He couldn't imagine Lianna being one to carry a gun if she didn't know how to use it.

He might not trust the doctor, but if the man had something to do with this whole mess, he wanted information from Lianna. Not to hurt her. Surely he wouldn't be dumb enough to hurt her with Reece right outside.

"All right," Reece agreed, still reluctant. Which he figured fit the profile of who he was pretending to be anyway. He lowered his voice as if he was trying to keep what he was going to say a secret from Dr. Winston. "I'd stay where I can see you, if I were you," he said, with enough threat and a cold look in his eyes to make it look like he really was some kind of pushy abuser.

"Of course," she said meekly.

But she had a gun strapped to her hip. She wasn't meek. She was here because she wanted to fight for her life. For her son's life. So Reece had to give her the space to do it.

And make sure this ended the way they both wanted.

Chapter Seventeen

"Can I get you some coffee?" Lianna didn't have to feign the nerves that made her look ineffectual and weak. This was all so strange. Pretending to be who she'd once been wasn't easy. It left a sick feeling in her gut, and she wanted to explain it to Dr. Winston. He'd been such a help to her.

But Reece was right. This was…strange, at best. If she listened to her gut as Shay had told her to, this was all wrong.

He should have called ahead. He shouldn't be here at all. But he stood in her entryway and she'd let Reece leave her alone with him.

He's your therapist. You don't actually think he's dangerous.

But that was the kind of thing she'd said to herself about Todd. *He's your husband. He doesn't mean it. He's the father of your child. He just needs time.*

She'd never had to remind herself that Reece or Shay or Sabrina had been there to help her. To keep her safe. Her doubts had been the little voice in her head. She rubbed at her temple. Trusting any kind of instincts was a lot harder than Shay had made it sound.

"Where's Henry?" Dr. Winston asked, that pleasant smile affixed to his face. He still held the travel bag clutched in his hand.

Lianna tried to keep her expression passive, but the mention of Henry had all those doubts souring into full-fledged distrust. *Maybe* she could reason away him asking about Henry if it had been summer break, but if things were normal, Henry should have been in school. And wouldn't Dr. Winston default to normal?

Maybe he thinks you're already on summer break. Maybe he wants to make sure you're sane enough to send him to school.

The problem was, she hadn't talked to this man since she'd moved to Echo. There'd been no check-ins. She hadn't even *wanted* to call him, like she'd been afraid she would. Moving to Echo had been good for her and Henry. Running the Bluebird had been everything she'd needed.

So what had brought him here now? What about now made him curious about Henry?

Should she lie? She tried to smile as if she still trusted the man before her. The man she'd told her problems to. Who'd taught her breathing exercises and helped her deal with her anxiety after Todd's death. He'd been good for her. She didn't think she would have been able to move away and find this place without his help.

But she couldn't settle into that old trust. Not with him *here* asking about Henry.

"Lianna?"

"I'm sorry. This is just kind of strange." She locked her fingers together, but let the tremor in them show. Trying to be brave while showing signs of nerves would work for this role she was playing. She hoped. She forced an anemic smile. "And you never answered me about the coffee."

"No, I'm fine. Why don't we sit?" He smiled genially, like he always had. Like he had always put her at ease.

Wasn't this the kind of paranoia he'd warned her against? That being isolated and alone would give rise to the environment where everything would feel fishy, wrong and potentially dangerous.

Then she thought about Reece. He'd been sent here, he'd come back with her, *because* things were dangerous. She'd felt that paranoia rise when he'd been staying here, *because* there'd been something to be paranoid about.

Still, she smiled and nodded at Dr. Winston and led him into the living room. He sat down on the big couch and placed his bag at his feet. The couch was big enough that the polite thing to do would be to sit next to him.

She decided instead to take a seat at the table where she had an old computer guests could use. It created a barrier between them and also made her feel less self-conscious about the gun strapped to her hip.

Dr. Winston sat comfortably on the couch, looking much like he had back in his office in Denver. A well-dressed man with a kind face and easy demeanor. Lianna figured he could make himself comfortable anywhere. Make himself seem like he was the authority in any room.

Even having her suspicions and doubts, she felt like she *had* to tell him everything.

But she didn't. She *wouldn't*.

"I realize it's…unorthodox of me to show up here," he said kindly. "But you know I had concerns about your move. As a mental health professional, I've found it hard to let that go. I wanted to check up on you, Lianna. And I have to say, I don't like what I see."

Nor should he, considering she was pretending to be a different version of herself. Guilt tried to win over, but she caught sight of Reece outside, peering into Dr. Winston's car. A reminder she wasn't in this alone.

"Letting another man take over your life, much like the last one did. And where did you say Henry was?"

Lianna outright frowned at Dr. Winston. This was all wrong. Guilt or doubts, in her gut, she knew Dr. Winston being here wasn't normal. Asking her about Henry…

Why was he asking about *Henry*? She'd taken Henry to see Dr. Winston once, and Henry had begged to never go back. Lianna had given in to Henry because Dr. Winston had made her leave the room, and no matter how much she trusted Dr. Winston, she didn't like the feeling of being separated from her son when he was so young, so vulnerable.

It hadn't been right, and she hadn't made Henry

go back because, overall, the death of his father hadn't changed his life. And he wasn't the one who'd been fooled. *She* was the one who'd needed therapy.

But Dr. Winston had always asked, applying a certain amount of pressure to bring Henry back. Oftentimes she'd leave his office thinking she would, but back home, faced with how well Henry was doing, she'd change her mind.

Why had he been so concerned about Henry? At the time she'd convinced herself it was professional courtesy or interest, but now…why was he asking after Henry again?

She looked up at Dr. Winston, and everything she'd been thinking must have been clear on her face, because his voice hardened.

"Lianna…? Where is he? I know he's not in Denver."

Lianna's heart stuttered, then thudded hard against her chest. In her ears. Her voice wasn't as calm as she would have liked. "How do you know that? *Why* do you know that?"

"Time is running out. I could have played this game for a lot longer if you'd kept your mouth shut. But you had to go get involved with people who would speed things up. I'm not a bad man, but you're forcing my hand."

Lianna slowly slid her hand toward the gun on her hip. Dr. Winston spoke so *rationally*, but the words weren't right. They didn't make sense. *He* didn't make sense. Her heart pounded as she nudged the shirt up so she could reach under and get her fingers around the gun handle.

He stood now, the color slowly rising in his face. Eyes cold and furious. "You told me you didn't know anything. I told them you didn't know anything, and now I'm being held responsible for your lies. It won't stand."

She wanted to look out the window at Reece, but she figured that would send the wrong message to Dr. Winston. *To them.* There was a "them" he was telling things to. It didn't sound like he was a part of what Todd had been doing, but Reece had been right. Dr. Winston had become a target.

Now he was blaming her for it.

She might have felt bad, confessed all, told Dr. Winston Reece could protect him, but the fury in his gaze stopped her. His obsession with Henry stopped her.

He stalked toward the table. Lianna's hands fumbled with the holster, but she didn't let that get to her. She just kept working it until she got the gun free.

Dr. Winston slapped his palms on the desk and leaned in toward her. "Where is Henry?"

THE GOOD DOCTOR had left his slick sports car unlocked, so Reece could get inside to search it with no problem. He glanced at the house. It was hard to see through the windows with the sunlight reflecting off them, but through the big picture windows he could see the doctor's legs. He was sitting on the couch, though his upper body was out of view. Lianna was somewhere hidden by the light's reflection.

He didn't like it. Even after the phone conversation with Elsie, when she assured him she'd dig everything up on Dr. Winston and get back to Reece ASAP, he didn't like being this far away. The doctor could as soon take out a gun and shoot Lianna in the head.

But Reece fought back the urge to run inside. He was a trained operative. He had to think like one. Not like a man...who felt the things he felt for Lianna.

The rational side of his brain understood it made no sense for someone to come this far only to kill Lianna. It made no sense for one person to be behind all of this. It made no sense...

Unless he needs to silence what she knows...

Before Reece could react to that horrible thought, he heard the *snick* of a footstep too close. He didn't pause or think. He acted out of instinct like he'd been trained to do practically his whole life. He whirled in the nick of time to keep a blow from knocking him out completely. Still, the meaty fist hit him in the shoulder and had him stumbling to the side.

He kept his balance, immediately squaring off to fight. He wasn't thrilled to find two men dressed in black materializing from the woods to join the man who'd taken the first blow.

"Three against one aren't great odds," the large man who'd swung at him said with a grin. Which deepened when the two men who'd joined him trained their high-powered automatic rifles on Reece's chest.

"I guess that depends," Reece replied, calculating his moves. He had a gun, but he'd have to unholster it, raise it and shoot before they pulled their triggers. And that wasn't just unlikely—it was impossible.

Especially considering their rifles were much more powerful than his pistol.

Three here. He used his peripheral vision to try to get a line of sight on Lianna. Were there more inside? Or had Dr. Winston underestimated Lianna enough to take her one-on-one?

God, he hoped so.

Lianna's cameras wouldn't pick up anything this far away from the house, so North Star wouldn't know he'd been compromised. They'd be able to at least *hear* something fishy in the living room with Lianna and the doctor, but it was very possible Dr. Winston knew that.

Everything was a little too possible.

"Well?" Reece asked of the three men just *standing* around, trying to look threatening. "Are you going to shoot me or what?"

The two with guns exchanged a look, and it was then Reece noticed they had earpieces in. Which spoke of more men. An organized team.

Though he swore internally, he leaned back casually on the car. He flashed a careless grin. "Waiting for orders, boys? That's not going to end well for you." The big one who'd tried to knock him out didn't appear to be armed, so Reece focused his attention on the two men with guns.

They held themselves alert, and the guns were pointed at him, but he noted they did not have their fingers curled around the trigger.

They weren't supposed to kill him. At least not without orders from their earpieces.

Reece didn't plan to wait for them to get any such directive.

Without warning or preamble or any more waiting, he lunged. A shot went off, but he didn't feel any bolt of pain as he'd expected. Which gave him all the opportunity he needed. He grabbed on to the gun he'd been lunging for, sweeping out his legs as he slid across the ground, tripping the other man with a gun.

His only goal was the two guns. Not inflicting damage. Not causing pain. Just get the guns. He could survive everything else these three men could dish out. He jerked the gun he'd lunged for out of the man's hands with a simple elbow to the throat and a tug timed perfectly.

They weren't well-trained muscle, that much was for sure. At best, Reece figured they were probably really good at shooting people and looking intimidating, but they didn't hold a candle to him when it came to hand-to-hand combat.

Lucky for him.

The man he'd tripped had fallen to the ground, but he still had the gun in his grasp and was fumbling to get back to his feet.

Reece swung out and used the butt of the gun he now held to land a nasty blow to the gun-wielding man's temple. He crumpled to the ground.

But Reece didn't have a chance to grab the other gun as the large man tackled him from behind, sending him and the gun sprawling.

The big guy made up for lack of technique with sheer size. He was all bulky muscle, a heavyweight who easily pinned Reece to the ground. He used one meaty hand to shove Reece's head into the dirt below, using his other hand and huge body to keep Reece's hands squeezed to his sides.

Which wasn't smart. He should have tried to cut off Reece's breathing, or rolled him over and started doling out some punches. God knew those ham fists could do some damage.

Reece struggled to breathe as his face was pressed into the soft earth, but all he needed was one perfect blow. One the man clearly wasn't expecting. He couldn't get his hands free, but his legs were mostly unencumbered. His aim had to be perfect, though, or no doubt Reece would be up a creek without a paddle.

He struggled against the dirt enough to keep the man's attention on him, but not enough to lose his breath. He focused, waited and then lifted the heel of his boot to hit the man in his most vulnerable place.

The man howled, and was surprised enough to let up on Reece's head, giving Reece a chance to wriggle and kick himself free.

Reece got to his feet, breathing too hard. His eyesight was slightly blurry from the pieces of mud stuck to his eyebrows and eyelashes. He tried to blink the obstructions away and assess the situation.

The big man was on his feet, though still huffing and puffing and holding on to his crotch. The guns were equally distant from the both of them.

A loud crash had both of them looking at the house. Lianna stumbled out and onto the porch. She had her gun in her hand, but Reece didn't get the impression she knew how to use it. Or at least not well enough to pick off the man he was fighting, from that distance.

Then Dr. Winston stumbled out after her. He looked injured, but not injured enough.

"Run," Reece yelled at her, ducking a fist and taking a few shuffle steps back to balance on one leg and sweep out with the other.

He didn't have the opportunity to watch and make sure she'd listened, because the big man was about to pick up one of the discarded guns, and that could *not* happen.

Chapter Eighteen

Reece had told her to run, so Lianna ran. Into the woods. Woods she'd played in as a child and still knew like the back of her hand.

Sabrina and Holden were placed somewhere in these woods, but in her hurry to escape Dr. Winston, she couldn't think about getting to them. She could only think about getting away.

Because he didn't want her. He wanted Henry.

How could he want Henry? Why would he be after her son? It didn't make sense, but she knew she couldn't allow him to get to her. He could use her as leverage—against Reece, against her grandparents. He could use her in a million ways she couldn't let happen. Not with Henry at stake.

So she ran. Zigzagging through the trees, jumping over fallen logs, skidding and sliding through the wet earth. Her heart thundered in her ears and her breath came in gasping pants that made her chest feel on fire.

She hadn't been able to shoot Dr. Winston, and she considered that a failing. He'd demanded information on Henry's whereabouts, but he hadn't actually grabbed her or tried to hurt her. Just intimidate her. So she hadn't been able to bring herself to get off a shot. She'd simply jumped up from the table and punched him. Giving her enough time to run away.

Then Reece had told her to run and she didn't know what else to do. He'd been fighting more men. Men with guns. She didn't think those men were here just to intimidate her.

Her pace slowed for a second as she thought of Reece. How would he fight off men with *guns*?

He can take care of himself. He told you to run.

She repeated those words to herself as she upped her pace again. She couldn't slow or look behind her, not when Dr. Winston had been so close. Maybe he wouldn't hurt her.

But maybe he would. It sure sounded like whoever he was involved with would. Because he said *someone* was demanding answers. Answers about Henry she wouldn't give. Ever.

"That'll be enough."

Lianna let out a short scream and slid to an inelegant stop as a man appeared in front of her, a large gun pointed right at her.

She didn't recognize him. Had no idea who he was or who he belonged to. But he had a much bigger gun than she did.

He gestured at her gun with his own. "Drop it."

She considered it. She also considered shooting him just to see if she could pull the trigger first. Whoever he was.

But she heard pounding footsteps and looked over

her shoulder to see Dr. Winston huffing and puffing behind her.

She was trapped. A gun pointed at her. A man behind her.

Keep calm. You can find a way out of this. Keep your head. Reece is out there. Sabrina and Holden are out here. Be calm. Be smart.

She only had to worry about staying alive.

"*This* is what you thought deserved protecting?" the man said, raising an eyebrow at Dr. Winston behind her.

"She's an innocent bystander," Dr. Winston bit out.

"Then I blame myself for thinking you understood that *innocence* doesn't matter here. Not with this."

Lianna stood very still. She did not drop her gun. Maybe this new man and Dr. Winston would get into some sort of argument and she'd be able to… do something.

But a shot rang out, so loud it drowned out the sound of her own scream. She dropped to her knees, thinking it must have hit her.

But she didn't hurt. She looked up. The man with the gun wasn't hurt, either. Sickly dread curdled in her stomach as she looked over her shoulder.

Dr. Winston lay crumpled on the ground. Completely and utterly still. Lianna closed her eyes against a wave of grief. Perhaps Dr. Winston hadn't been a good man, but he hadn't shot at her, either. He'd called her an innocent bystander, and now…

"I'm going to suggest that when you get back up

to your feet, you leave the gun on the ground. If you don't…well…"

Lianna swallowed down the grief and the fear and brought her gaze to the man standing in front of her. "You need me," Lianna managed to say. "You can't kill me."

The man snorted. "This isn't a movie. I can kill you whenever I feel like it and get the information I want elsewhere. But it'll be far more fun to torture the information out of you. To watch you give me everything I want to know, and then realize you'll die anyway. And so will your son."

Though fear drummed through her, she sneered at the man threatening her. "You'll never touch my son."

The man moved toward her. He was tall and very broad. He looked like an athlete of some kind. Not menacing or evil like bad guys in a movie. He looked more like the dopey football star she'd gone to high school with.

But his words were cold and cruel, and so were his blue eyes as he crouched in front of her, still with the gun pointed at her chest. "Maybe your dead husband shouldn't have been so loose-lipped around a kid."

"Henry doesn't know anything." Her voice shook. *Everything* shook. At least she was sitting, so her legs couldn't give out. What the armed man had forgotten about or didn't seem to care about was the fact she still had her hand on her gun.

Not as big or high-powered as his, and she certainly was no great shot, but he was right there. In front of her.

The man smiled. "Doesn't he?"

Lianna's throat was dry, and swallowing didn't help. Still, she tried to hold on to her last sliver of calm and authority. Because she was Henry's mother, and she'd save him from this. No matter what it took. "Tell me what you think he knows."

"Yes, of course. I'll tell you my whole plan. I'll talk and talk and talk until your friends show up and take me away. Saving you. Are you kidding?"

Todd had taken that tone with her on occasion. It had always felt as much like a physical slap as anything else. She'd cowered when he'd make her feel like he knew so much more than her.

She wasn't that Lianna anymore. "Are you?" she returned, and lifted the gun and shot.

THE BIG MAN Reece was grappling with simply wouldn't go down. Reece had managed to wrestle him to the ground before he'd reached the gun, but all they'd managed to do was roll and roll and exchange painful punches.

At least Reece had been able to roll him away from the guns. Hand to hand… Well, maybe he wouldn't win, but at least he wouldn't die.

The man made a tactical error, giving Reece the upper hand. It took time, and all of his strength, but Reece managed to choke him until the man blacked out, going still.

Tentatively, Reece backed away. Inch by inch, until he was up on his feet and the man was still on the ground, immobile.

He heard footsteps again, inwardly swore, then

whirled around, ready to fight. But it was Holden. "What are you doing here?"

"Trying to meet up with Sabrina, but we lost communication. Guess you handled this," Holden said, gesturing at the three motionless men on the ground.

Reece didn't even bother to respond to that. There was no time. He took off in the direction Lianna had gone.

He heard Holden running behind him, hissing his name in an attempt to be somewhat tactical, but screw tactics. Reece had to get to Lianna.

"Reece. Wait. That doctor? He wasn't after Lianna." Holden ran after Reece. Reece didn't slow down, but he did listen.

"What do you mean?"

"Elsie was listening in on the conversation. He wanted Henry. *Demanded* Henry. But he didn't hurt Lianna. Didn't even really threaten her. Just demanded the information for the people he was working for."

Reece nearly ran into a tree as he turned to look at Holden in surprise, sure he'd misheard. "What?"

"Henry. It was all he would talk about. He wanted Henry. Reece, is there any chance Henry knows… something?"

Reece wanted to deny it, but hadn't he had a feeling…an inkling when Henry had asked him to keep Lianna safe, that the boy understood more than they thought? Lianna had waved it off, and Reece had, too. Perhaps because they both didn't want to believe…

"We need to find out what Henry knows."

"Shay and Betty are on it."

"They have to be gentle with him," Reece said, sick with the idea the kid was doing this alone. Without Lianna. Without him. "He's just a kid. I think he's scared…"

"I'm sure they get it, Reece. He's a good kid. No one's going to intimidate him. Not in our group. Besides, Lianna's grandpa is there."

Reece nodded mechanically. Logically he understood that, but his chest still ached at the fact Henry would have to sit there and answer questions without him or Lianna there to…to protect him. Help him.

"Find Sabrina. Three men after me. One man after Lianna. We don't know who else is out there. I know someone was feeding orders to the goons I took on. If Henry knows who's behind all this, we need to make sure our next target is the leader…not just the muscle after us."

"On it. I'll go back to Sabrina's initial point, fan out from there till I find her. You're going after the doctor?"

"I'm going after Lianna. She's priority number one."

Holden didn't say anything to that. He simply peeled off to the west, where Sabrina had initially been planted. Reece tracked Lianna's route. The wet earth made her footprints and sliding slips in the mud easy to track at a decent pace.

The sound of a gunshot echoing through the trees had Reece's heart jumping to his throat.

Lianna.

HENRY COULDN'T CONCENTRATE on the arcade game. His head was fuzzy and he missed Mom. His stomach felt like a big fat rock. He chewed on his lip and looked back at Great-Grandpa.

Gramps was sitting on a big comfy chair in the corner, reading one of his big, boring books. He didn't like the arcade games, but he always stopped reading to play with him if Henry asked.

Henry didn't feel much like playing with anybody today. Not with Mom and Reece gone. No one would tell him everything. He didn't know *what* was going on, but he knew it wasn't good.

It made him think about his dad. It made him think about secrets. He tried to never think about either.

He heard voices in the hall, and his stomach hurt even more. Shay and Betty walked in, and their eyes were on him. Henry backed away from both of them.

"Henry." Betty's voice was kind and soft, but both she and Shay moved toward him. Henry scrambled back to Gramps.

"Did something happen?" Gramps demanded, putting his book down and getting up out of his chair.

"No, Mr. Young. Not exactly. We've received some information, though. We think if we get some answers, we might be able to figure some other things out before…"

Shay trailed off, and her gaze was on him again. Henry wanted to hide behind Gramps, but he couldn't seem to look away from Shay.

"Henry, do you know something about your dad that you haven't told us?"

Gramps slid his arm around Henry's shoulders.

Henry wished it made him feel brave. But the rock in his stomach was getting bigger, making him feel sick.

"He's a boy," Gramps said, pulling Henry behind him. "Why would you question a little boy?" he demanded, his voice as angry as Henry had ever heard it.

Henry closed his eyes.

"Mr. Young, we think Henry knows something. Something important. Something that could help us keep Lianna safe. We don't want to scare Henry. We just want to ask a few questions."

But Henry was scared. Scared of everything. He kept his eyes closed and his head pushed into Gramps's back. He'd just stay here until they went away. Until it all went away.

"Henry." It was Betty's voice, and Henry felt her soft hand on his elbow. "Sweetie. I know everything is pretty scary right now, but we only want to help. Is there something you need to tell us?"

Henry blinked his eyes open. Betty was looking at him earnestly. Her hand was soft and reassuring on his elbow. Gramps still held him. He was safe here. Mom had brought them here to be safe.

Maybe that meant… "I'm not supposed to tell," Henry whispered. There were tears in his eyes, but he was strong. Like Reece. He'd be strong for Mom and he wouldn't cry.

"Why not, honey?" Betty asked. He liked Betty. She was…soft, but really good at stuff. Like Mom.

"They'll hurt her."

Betty looked up at Shay. Henry could tell Shay didn't like that answer and he hunched even more toward Gramps. Angry eyes. He recognized those all too well. They happened before the yelling. Dad always had angry eyes. And always yelled.

Henry wasn't sorry he was dead, like some people told him he was. Everything was better since Dad had been gone. No more angry eyes.

Reece was never angry. Sometimes he even looked kind of sad. But Shay looked *very* angry right now. Still, she didn't shout like Dad.

She didn't grab him like his father had that one time.

Your mother will die if you breathe a word of this to anyone ever. Do you understand me?

"Honey, I need you to tell me everything you know about what's going on." Betty smoothed a hand over his hair, just like Mom did when he had a nightmare. "Anything about your dad. I know you're afraid. But you know we're doing everything in our power to protect your mom, and this will help."

Reece was with Mom. And Sabrina and Holden. He trusted Reece the most, but Sabrina was pretty cool. And Holden looked strong. They'd all been nice, and they helped.

Betty was nice. Betty was *kind*, and she wanted to help him. Dad was dead. Maybe…maybe he could tell.

"Dad worked for a bad man named Gene Handler." Henry didn't know what to make of the way the adults reacted to that. They all got really, really still.

Henry huddled deeper into himself. "They were selling guns to bad guys. Dad got jobs with good organizations, stole guns, then gave them to Gene."

"Henry," Betty breathed. "How do you know this?"

"I accidentally heard it." He looked up at all the adults in the room. They didn't look angry anymore. So he figured he could keep going. "I couldn't sleep one night and I went to sneak some candy from the pantry. I had my flashlight and I went inside the pantry. I closed the door and got my candy and started to eat it there. But then I heard Dad. He was talking to someone."

Henry remembered how scared he'd been he was going to get in trouble. Then how scared at what Dad had been saying to a man named Gene.

"They argued, and Dad said he'd handle everything. Dad called him Gene once and then Handler once, so I figured that was the guy's name. They talked about guns. At first I thought they were maybe talking about Mature video games, but then I knocked a box off the pantry shelf."

Gramps's arm tightened around him, and Betty smoothed down his hair again, so Henry kept going.

"Dad jerked open the door. The bad man was gone, but Dad was mad. He…" Henry was telling the truth, but maybe he didn't need to tell the whole truth.

"He hurt you?" Betty said, and it didn't feel like a question. It felt like Betty knew. So Henry nodded.

"He picked me up by my shirt. He shook me. He said if I ever said anything to anyone, Mom would die. I didn't think they were talking about video games anymore."

The entire room was silent. The air felt heavy. Henry wanted to cry, but he blinked back the tears. *Be strong like Reece.*

Shay turned and walked out of the room. Henry felt his whole body tremble.

"Am I in trouble?" he managed to ask, even though his throat felt too tight.

"No, baby. No," Betty said. "You just… You are very, very brave and I am so proud of you." Betty smiled at him, but her eyes were bright. "Shay and Elsie are going to work really hard to bring your mom back. Today."

"And Reece?"

Betty drew him into a fierce hug. "Definitely."

Chapter Nineteen

Lianna still held the gun up, but she had her eyes squeezed shut. Which was so incredibly dangerous. She'd shot the gun and nothing on her hurt except her hand and her ears.

Which meant she had to have hit him. Which meant she had to open her eyes and figure out what to do.

It took considerable time to talk herself up to it. To get over the panic and the fear and what she supposed must be shock, as a weird, foggy numbness settled over her.

But this wasn't over. Even if she didn't want to see what damage she'd done to another human being, there were still men Reece was fighting. She still had to get home and safe to Henry.

She managed to open her eyes. Her breath came in short, panicked bursts no matter how well she knew she needed to calm down.

The man she'd shot lay on the ground right where he'd been crouching. She didn't see where he'd been shot, and she could see the rise and fall of his chest. So he wasn't dead.

A new fear filtered through the shock, but still she sat on the wet earth with the gun clutched in her hand, pointing it at someone who wasn't upright anymore.

He *had* to have been shot if he was lying there. He'd been *right* in front of her, so she couldn't have missed.

Run, her mind screamed. *Find Reece. Get out of here.*

The gunshot was still echoing in her head, and she wavered. Should she shoot him again? This unknown man. He'd threatened Henry, but could she...kill?

Just run away.

She managed to get to her feet, though her vision blurred and her balance was off. Shock. Panic. She had to shake them all away and focus on the fact she was fine.

Not that she'd probably killed a man.

She took a deep breath and looked around the woods. Which way had she come from? Which way did she need to go? Everything looked the same, and all those landmarks she usually kept track of on a walk were jumbled in her head.

It didn't matter which way she went, as long as she went. Whether she got back to the inn or walked through the woods until she got to the road, it was better than staying here when the man was still breathing.

Still breathing, and he had a gun. She needed to take it—not just to protect herself, but to protect everyone in these woods. He wasn't holding it any-more, but he was half lying on it. It was possible if she pulled it out from under him he'd wake up. She didn't know how gunshot wounds worked, but she doubted it would knock him out unless it was bad. Unless he was dying.

She should just grab the gun and run. That was what she had to do. She inched closer to the man. She held her own gun pointed at him so that if he moved, she could shoot. She could protect herself.

She grabbed the end of the gun that wasn't hidden under the man's torso and pulled. At first she tried to be gentle. Tried not to disturb whatever unconsciousness he was in, but as the gun refused to budge, she focused more on pulling harder and getting it out than being careful about it.

There was the sound of movement. Then a hand closed around her ankle. Lianna tried to jerk away, but the hand merely pulled as she tried to take off, sending her sprawling forward. She landed hard, a nasty face-plant that had her grip on the gun loosening and her teeth cracking against each other.

A heavy weight fell on top of her. The man. Pinning her to the ground. She struggled, but it was no use. "Did you think it'd be that easy?" he growled into her ear.

Lianna closed her eyes, reaching as hard as she could for the gun that she could still touch but wasn't close enough to wrap her fingers around.

"Oh, I don't think so." He reached over her head, with much longer arms than hers, and plucked the gun out of her grasp. She continued to struggle against his heavy weight. She kicked and wriggled and tried to push herself up out of the dirt.

The man wrenched her arm behind her back, and she howled at the shock of pain that went through her shoulder at the uncomfortable angle he had her arm at.

"Just wait."

Reece. Reece's voice. Calm and authoritative over the sound of her struggle and own harsh breathing. She didn't look up. She was too afraid one move would get her killed before Reece could save her.

Then the man jerked her up out of the mud by her shirt, practically choking her in the process. But that thought was secondary to the fact there was now cold steel pressed to her temple.

"On your feet," the man seethed at her, still twisting one arm behind her back. She slid in the mud but managed to get unsteadily to her feet.

She looked at Reece now. He stood a few yards from them. His lip was bleeding, and she could tell there were places on his face that were already swelling and bruising. Still, he stood tall. He held a gun and looked like...

Her savior.

"We have the kid," Reece said, not making eye contact with her. "She wouldn't be able to get to him if she wanted to. You want the kid, it's me you're after."

"So I can kill her?" the man said, digging the gun harder against her temple.

Reece shrugged negligently. So nonchalantly Lianna didn't know how to believe he was acting. They had Henry. Was that what he'd wanted all along? *Fool you twice...*

"I mean, I don't know why you'd want that kind of cleanup," Reece said. "But that's your business." His voice was flippant, and Lianna…

Stop, she ordered herself. *Think.*

His gaze was steady on the man holding her. Steady and cold. His grip on the gun was tight. His entire posture was rigid, no matter how he shrugged. He'd fought off men with guns to get here. He was *injured*.

And he didn't look at her. Not because she didn't matter, but because she did. And what would a man like Reece do if she became collateral damage? He certainly wouldn't go back to his group and keep working. He wouldn't make sure Henry was okay. He'd simply…give up.

Which meant she had to help herself get out of this mess as much as she had to trust Reece to do the same.

REECE HAD LEARNED from a young age how to deal with terror. He'd grown so used to it, *this* terror was almost new. He didn't know how he'd survive it if Lianna's blood ended up on his hands.

"I didn't kill your guys. Just left them incapacitated for a bit."

"I don't care about those idiots," the man said. He held the gun to Lianna's temple, but Reece couldn't let himself look at her. If he made eye contact, he'd simply…break.

At this point, what he needed to do was keep the man's attention on him. Once Holden found Sabrina, they would be able to get here and take this guy out without hurting Lianna.

And if Holden disappears like Sabrina seems to have?

Only time would tell. He had to work this through one step at a time. "You want proof I got the kid?"

The man looked at him with narrowed eyes. Reece memorized his face. Square jaw, crooked nose. Blond hair, blue eyes, six-three give or take, and a very solid two-forty. He was built like a linebacker. But there was a trickle of blood running down his face.

Elsie hadn't been able to connect Dr. Winston to any groups, so they were still working blind on who they were fighting. But Reece would commit this man to memory and spend the rest of his damn life bringing him to justice if he had to.

If he got out of this alive. Because he'd do anything—including die—to get Lianna safe.

"You got proof?" the man said suspiciously.

"You let me get my phone out of my pocket, yeah, I got proof."

"Drop the gun."

"You can't honestly expect me to drop my gun. I gotta protect myself, man. I'm not here to hurt you. In fact, I'd be willing to take some kind of buyout. If whoever you're working for can afford me."

The man paused at that. Didn't seem to have anything to say. He wasn't wearing a headpiece like the men Reece had fought earlier had been. It could mean he was the leader, but Reece had a bad feeling he was dealing with another underling.

"I'll hold up my gun, pull out the phone, get the

kid on a video call. You just want confirmation or you want what he knows?"

Again, the man holding Lianna was silent, so Reece just kept moving forward. Waiting would give him too much time to think, to despair, to make a mistake where he put his need to get Lianna away from the gun over the reality that he wouldn't reach her in time.

He held up his gun, barrel up, palm toward the man. He pulled out his phone with his other hand and used his secure line to connect with Elsie.

When she appeared on his screen, Reece forced himself to curve his mouth into a smile. As if he was talking to a small boy. "Heya, Hank."

He heard Lianna sob and he had to push the sound away. Freeze it out. He looked at Elsie's face on his screen. She was scrambling with how to respond, clearly. Where was Shay?

"Hi, Reece," Elsie said in some horrible approximation of a child's voice. Reece didn't outwardly react. He doubted the man holding Lianna knew Henry from Adam. Hopefully he'd never met a seven-year-old boy before, either.

"I got a friend I need you to talk to," Reece said, sounding downright jovial.

Reece looked up at the man holding Lianna. The man looked suspicious, but he still stayed yards away from Reece, not reacting. Which was when Reece noticed the man's shirt was wet. It wasn't mud.

Blood. The shirt was a little torn. He'd heard two gunshots go off earlier. "You okay, buddy?" Reece said, nodding to the man's side. It was the side closest to Lianna.

For the first time, he dared look at her. She was pale, streaked with mud from her head to her toes. Her hair was a mess and there was terror in her blue eyes. But not just terror.

Determination.

"Looks nasty, doesn't it?" he said to her. "Maybe he'll let you check it out for him?"

"I don't need anyone to check it out," the man said. "Just grazed me. Show me the phone."

Reece moved slowly. Carefully. He didn't want to make any sudden movements, and he had to make sure it didn't look like he was calculating how to get Lianna out of his clutches even though he was.

"Stop."

Reece stopped on a dime. He held both hands up, though he made sure the phone screen was facing himself.

"Just toss me the phone."

"You're not going to catch it one-handed, bleeding like that," Reece assured him. He crouched carefully and placed the gun on the ground. If he got close enough, the guns wouldn't matter anyway. "Better?"

The man took his time to consider, which tested the last thread of patience Reece was hanging on to. But the gun was digging into Lianna's head, and there was *nothing* Reece could do to make that less of a real, horrible threat.

It wasn't right or fair that she should have to suffer through this. He had to make it end. Here. Now.

Even if it led to his own end.

Chapter Twenty

Lianna's mind was moving in a million different directions. The voice that had come out of the phone was assuredly *not* Henry, but the way Reece had said "Hank" like he usually did had practically cut her in two.

It was another act. So flippant and fake, as if Reece was ever any of those things. But that only reminded her she could put on an act, too.

"Please," she said, letting the fear and a whine into her voice. "Please, let me talk to him. Please. I have to talk to Henry. Please. Please."

The gun dug into her skin and Lianna winced.

"Shut up," the man said.

Reece continued to move very slowly toward the man. He'd mentioned the man was bleeding. Lianna couldn't see it out of her peripheral vision, but she thought if she could figure out where it was, maybe she could hit him there. Would he be able to pull the trigger before she finished trying to hurt him?

That was the part that kept her completely and utterly still. Reece kept moving toward them, the phone in his hand, the gun left behind.

Why had he left his gun behind?

He came to a stop in front of the man. She could have reached out and touched him. But he didn't look at her. He held out the phone.

Lianna inhaled. Now or never. Either she tried to help or she didn't. He was distracted by reaching out to grab the phone, so she acted.

Everything happened too quickly to fully place into a sequence of events. She knew she ducked and rammed into the man holding a gun to her head. She knew the gun went off, too close to her ears, but no matter the pain in them or how they rang, she hadn't been shot.

She stumbled away, took in the scene. Reece and the man wrestled on the ground, and she knew somewhere in the back of her head that Reece was yelling at her to run. Again.

She'd run last time and it had led her here. Running wasn't a good idea. She had to fight somehow.

Reece and the man rolled and grunted. The man still had his gun and Reece was trying to get out of his grasp. Lianna crept forward, moving for Reece's gun. She couldn't shoot the man while he was rolling around with Reece, but maybe she'd get the opportunity. Maybe she could shoot the gun in the air and create a diversion.

Reece managed to get to his feet, but the man was right behind him. Still, it gave Lianna her chance.

She pulled the trigger, but the man didn't go down. His arm jerked, though. Before she could determine if she'd hit him, Reece pushed her back and she stumbled, hitting the ground with a bone-rattling crash as another gunshot went off.

This time, she held on to the gun, and immediately pointed it at the man again. He was switching guns from one arm to the other, since the hand holding his gun was now a bloody mess. She *had* shot him there.

He glared at her. "You're one terrible—"

Before he got the rest of the sentence out of his mouth, she pulled the trigger again. This time, the man went down.

Lianna whirled to find Reece. He was sprawled on the ground, breathing ragged as he seemed to be trying to drag himself toward her. But he couldn't manage.

Oh no.

Lianna dropped to the ground next to him. "Reece."

He made a noise, but it was an awful noise. "I'm okay," he said, but the words were gritted out and thready at best. "It's okay."

"Reece…" She tried to help him up, but he was too heavy and wasn't trying to get up himself. "Reece, where are you hurt?"

He exhaled in huffs, as if trying to breathe through a pain, but from her vantage point, she had no idea… That was when he rolled over onto his back and she could see the tear of his shirt, the terrifying spurts of blood. So much blood. And a bullet wound, right below his rib cage, that left little to the imagination.

Dizziness threatened but she bit down on her tongue. She had to be brave and figure out what to do about this horrible, horrible thing. Her hands shook but she touched his face. "Shh. It's okay." What should she do? Pressure. They put pressure on wounds in movies. Did she trust a movie? "It's okay," she repeated, because maybe if she said it enough times she'd believe it.

"I'm not so sure about that," Reece gritted out. "Lianna. Get out of here. I don't know what happened to Holden and Sabrina. I don't know... Get out of here. Keep Henry safe. Okay?"

His words were harder and harder to understand, gritted and slurred and *oh, God*. She rolled up the bottom of his shirt and forced herself to put all the pressure she could manage on his wound.

He groaned in pain, but he was going gray. "Reece. Stay right here. Everything is going to be okay."

"Of course it is," he gritted out, squeezing his eyes shut. "But if it's not, it's okay. Everything's okay. I love you."

Love.

A hand wrapped around her arm and Lianna immediately fought it away, pushing and punching against the person who grabbed her.

"Hey. It's okay. It's okay. Lianna. Look at me."

It finally broke through her panic and fear about the blood that it was Holden grabbing her, talking to her.

"Where were you?" she demanded, tears filling her eyes against her will. "Help him."

"We already called in a medic team. Sabrina knows some basic field medicine."

Lianna looked at Reece, and finally realized Sabrina was here, too. Her face was all bloody and she held her arm at an odd angle, but there was no trace of pain in her expression. Only grim determination as she used her good arm to check Reece's pulse, then press a lump of cloth, which Holden handed her, to Reece's bloody chest.

"What happened?"

"She got ambushed by a couple guys," Holden said. When Lianna looked at him, he was checking the pulse of the man who'd shot Reece. He dropped the man's arm and stood. "We took care of them. Just took some time." She could hear the guilt in Holden's tone. Because if something happened to Reece, it was all their fault. "More people coming. Medics. Cleanup."

"He's dead?"

Holden nodded.

Dead. She'd killed a man. The man who'd killed Dr. Winston, the man who'd wanted to kill her. Who might have killed Reece.

She looked at him. If Reece died, wouldn't that be two lives on her conscience? He couldn't die. He couldn't. Lianna crawled back to his side.

"Is he going to be okay?" Lianna asked Sabrina.

Sabrina looked up at Lianna grimly. "I don't know."

Lianna closed her eyes and ran her hand over his hair, his cheek, whispering encouraging things. Anything she could think of. "I love you, too. So you have to live. You have to fight. You have to come back to me and Henry. You have to."

The words kept tumbling out of her mouth long after the medics arrived and took him away.

REECE HAD BEEN here before. In the dark. In pain, or worse, that floaty place where there was no pain. No nothing. Except sometimes memories. Of his parents. Of fear.

Of all the ways he'd tried to make up for what bad his parents had done.

Sometimes he heard Lianna's voice, but it must have been a hallucination, because she'd murmured things about love and taking care of him forever, and that was a dream. Not reality.

But they still made him want…more. More than the darkness. More than the pain.

He came in and out in waves. Sometimes he wasn't sure what was real and what was a dream. Surely Sabrina offering tearful apologies for being too late was a dream? Shay scolding him for not following protocol probably wasn't.

But more often than not, when he thought he opened his eyes, it was Lianna's blue eyes staring back. Warm and loving. And tired.

This time when he woke up, he felt…almost real. No fuzzy dream world. There was a sharp pain right below his rib cage, and there were the annoying beeping sounds he associated with hospitals. The lights seemed too bright and he blinked against them, but closing his eyes didn't send him back into the dark.

That was something. He wasn't sure how long it took him to come to full consciousness. Aware of his surroundings, his body and his own thoughts. This wasn't the first time he'd been shot or injured. He'd had his fair share.

But this was the first time he'd woken up and known there was something...and *someones*...waiting for him.

He looked over at the woman sitting next to his bed. Her eyes were assessing, and she didn't say anything. Just sat there, arms crossed.

"Shay."

"Don't sound so disappointed."

"Everything's okay? Everyone? Bring me up to speed." Everything was a scramble. He'd stopped the bullet from hitting Lianna, hadn't he? She'd gotten away? Henry was safe and...

"This'll be the third time I do that. Think it'll stick this time around?"

Reece tried to shift in his bed, but it sent a wave of pain through him. "How long have I been in here?" he muttered.

"Day five, buddy. But you seem about as alert as I've seen you. Gunshot nicked some organs in there. Surgery's no joke on that. On top of blood loss and the like. But you'll live."

"Well, I guess that's something. Lianna and Henry..."

"Safe and sound. For good. The small weapons distributor Todd Kade was involved with has been taken out. All dead or arrested. They were only out for Henry because he could ID their head guy, thanks to dad of the year. Won't matter now. They basically identified themselves with all this, and what we couldn't pin on them the shrink had kept a record of in his journal. He's the only casualty outside of the weapons dealers."

Reece let his fuzzy brain work through that. Lianna and Henry safe and sound, and for good. The ghost of Todd Kade laid to rest.

"Holden and Sabrina?"

"Banged up, but on the mend. You're the only idiot who jumped in front of a bullet."

Reece let out a breath. The whole thing was hazy, and he didn't fully remember jumping in front of anything, but he knew the feeling that had gone through him. "Couldn't let it be her."

"Yeah. Well, you're okay and getting better now. I know you've all been worried about North Star going under, but we're not going anywhere. This has opened up a new case for us. We've got some weapons to find for our new friends. So you have to get better and fast. We're going to need you." She smiled, but he could see the worry around the edges. The fear. Being this injured had affected their unflappable leader. Just like when Granger had been hurt.

Because North Star was a family. They had become his family. He wasn't sure he'd ever have admitted that to himself if he hadn't flirted with death there for a few minutes. Or days. Whatever it had been. But he cared about each member.

And they cared about him.

But that didn't mean North Star was his life anymore. Even if he could heal as fast as Shay wanted him to—which he doubted, based on all the machines attached to him—he didn't *want* to. "I'm not taking any more assignments, Shay."

"I know you're going to have to be out for a few weeks. Obviously, you'll take your time and get all healed up. Then you'll be good as new, and when you're ready—"

"No, I'm done. Really done." He knew people would doubt him. He was laid up in a hospital bed, after all. Probably pumped full of drugs. But he knew it in his heart. In his soul. "I don't want to fight anymore. I want…"

Shay was very still and looked at him with perhaps a little too much understanding. "A family?"

"Yeah." He'd never thought he'd want something so simple, but he'd never known what family was. Until Lianna and Henry had shown him.

"You don't think you'll miss it?"

Miss it? He'd joined North Star after the army because he'd had a need to…help. To ease something inside of himself. It was never about the *work*. "I've been fighting my whole life. For survival. Then to help people, hoping to fill that hole of never being helped myself. But the only thing that's ever come close is…love. I guess."

Shay snorted. "You *guess*."

"I've survived. I've helped a lot of people. At some point… At some point there's got to be more than that."

"For some people," Shay said, standing.

"It's a young man's game, Shay. Even you can't do it forever. Look at Granger."

"He could do it if he wanted to," she said, a surprising amount of bitterness in her tone for someone who'd gotten to take over in his absence.

"Maybe that's the point. No one wants to forever." Reece closed his eyes against the wave of pain. Soon nurses would be in to inject something else into him, but he had things to say first. "I'm not sure I would have come to that conclusion if I hadn't been this hurt, hadn't had this much not-all-there time to realize… Everyone deserves a chance at a real life. Beyond assignments and missions. No one should have to pay someone else's penance forever." It was true. He'd been trying to make up for the bad his parents had to have done in their gang, but he'd never done it.

Because he couldn't live his life paying for mistakes that weren't his. He didn't feel that mantle of guilt and shame anymore. Not when he wanted something real for the first time in his life.

"Can you get Lianna in here before one of those nurses forces some more drugs on me?"

"She's right outside."

Maybe she hadn't been a dream or a hallucination. As Shay slid out the door and Lianna immediately entered the room, he realized it hadn't been. She'd been here the whole time.

She rushed over to him. She had on what he would call her mom smile. Indulgent but authoritative. "Well, hello there. It's good to see your eyes." She settled herself on the chair and didn't give him the chance to speak. "I'm going to need you to get well enough for them to move you into a room with less restrictions. Henry is beside himself that they won't let children in. School just isn't in the cards until you're better."

Reece frowned. "He should be back in school. Shay said it's safe. He should—"

"My grandfather has been keeping in touch with Henry's teacher, helping him do any work he needs to for the end of the year," she interrupted, popping back up to her feet. She straightened his blankets and the wires on his IV. "He worked everything out with the school, so he's essentially on early summer break without it affecting him adversely. Going home just isn't an option until you can go with us."

"Go with you," he echoed, watching her fiddle with his bed. He never would have believed he'd like someone fussing over him, but it warmed his heart.

"Yes, and I won't hear any arguing," she said primly. "You'll need to be taken care of, and I intend to be the one to do it. I owe you my life."

Ah, well, this all made sense now, didn't it? He shifted in his bed, wincing at the pain. When he spoke, it came out gruffer than he'd intended. "You don't owe me a damn thing."

"Now, now." She leaned over the bed, brushing her hand over his hair. "Don't get worked up."

If he could move right, he would have grabbed her hand and pulled her right on top of him. Show her how *worked up* he could be. But he didn't have that option, he supposed. "I'm not getting worked up. And I won't have you taking care of me because you feel guilty or…or like it's payback or…whatever. No, I won't."

She blinked, and the hand on his hair that had been so…*officious*…gentled. She cupped his cheek, studying his face. He didn't have a clue what he looked like, but it couldn't be good.

"I love you, Reece." She said it quietly and matter-of-factly. "So we'll be nursing you back to health for however long it takes, and we'll deal with the rest once you're well enough to…go back."

This time he did reach up and managed to encircle her wrist with his fingers, thick and clumsy as they felt. "I'm not going back."

"Don't be silly. You'll get better."

"Yes, but I'm not going back to North Star. I don't want to be a field operative anymore."

She sucked in a breath at that, and then let it out slowly. Watching him all the while. "What do you want?"

He thought for a long moment. In his whole life, there'd only ever been one thing he'd ever truly wanted. One thing he'd thought he'd never find. "Home."

She didn't say anything to that, though her eyes filled.

"You could probably use a hand around the inn. I'm handy. I can wash dishes, pick up groceries. I don't require much."

"No, I don't suppose you do." She sighed. "And what about love?"

"I'd give it," he said gruffly, not letting go of her hand.

"And take it?"

"I guess I'd have to."

She leaned closer, one hand still on his face, one

hand captured in his. She kept her gaze steady on his and said very seriously, "Yes, you would."

"Lianna, I only want to go home to you and Henry. It's all I want."

"It's all I want, too."

Epilogue

Everyone told Reece he'd change his mind. When he got out of the hospital, when he moved in with Lianna. North Star people, Lianna herself. Everyone.

Reece didn't miss it. Weeks out of the hospital, moved into the Bluebird, living with Henry and Lianna as a family… No, he'd never once looked back and missed his work as a field operative.

He fixed things that broke. He helped around the inn, getting groceries, making beds, greeting guests. He'd been roped into coaching Henry's baseball team, and he found the home he'd always wanted.

He loved Lianna and Henry, and built the life he hadn't known would have been possible a few short months ago.

But most of all, he didn't give up one family for the other. Even secret group operatives could take a break to see a kid's Little League game. As evidenced by the fact Shay and Betty were standing next to Lianna as he and Henry left the field after one of Henry's games.

"Where's Sabrina?" Henry asked, all but dancing on air. He'd gotten his first extra-base hit and hadn't come down from cloud nine.

"She's on assignment, but she'll be at the next game," Shay said, giving Henry a high five.

"But I'll send her video of your monster hit, Mr. Baseball," Betty added, slinging her arm around Henry's shoulders.

Henry grinned. "Cool."

"We've got to get back," Shay said to Lianna.

"You're not coming over for the barbecue?" Lianna asked. "You know you're both welcome. And you can take some leftovers to Holden and Sabrina."

Shay shook her head. "Both out on jobs. Next time we're in between assignments we'll be better, longer guests."

Reece nodded. "Well, you're always welcome."

Some of Henry's teammates came over and dragged him off to the playground. Betty and Lianna had their heads together about something, and Shay just looked at him, shaking her head.

"Can't say I ever predicted any of this, but it looks good on you, Reece."

"Yeah, it does."

"You're really not coming back, are you?"

"Really not."

She slapped him on the back. "Well, I guess I won't ask you to come back anymore. But if you ever change your mind…"

"I won't."

Shay smiled. "Yeah, well. See you later. Come on, Bet."

Shay and Betty left, and Lianna rounded up Henry so they could drive home. Reece barbecued dinner, and they ate together discussing the week ahead.

They had two couples coming for a stay, making for a busy week.

Henry ran off to play his hour of video games as Reece helped Lianna clear off the kitchen table.

"Did she ask you to come back?" Lianna asked lightly as she rinsed off dishes and placed them in the dishwasher.

Reece didn't have to ask who or what she meant. He came up behind her, wrapped his arms around her waist and rested his chin on her shoulder. "Yes."

"And you didn't feel the slightest twinge to agree?" she asked, and though her voice remained light, he could feel the tension within her.

"Not the slightest."

Her shoulders relaxed.

"Come on, Lianna. I thought we were past this."

"It isn't that. It's only…" She let out a breath, then laughed. She nudged him off her and turned to face him. She blew out a breath. "Reece, I'm pregnant."

He stood there, those words echoing in his ears for…he didn't know how long. He opened his mouth to speak, but his throat had tightened up. But Lianna had given him a few lessons along the way. Among them that even when he didn't have the words, he could reach out and find someone to hold.

Which was what he did. Pulled her into his arms. Buried his face in her shoulder. Held her tight until he knew what to say. "We have to get married."

She pushed him away, but he didn't budge, just pulled his head back to look at her. "You said you wanted to wait a year."

"I didn't want to. I thought we should, but now?

No. We'll get married. Then we can do the adoption paperwork for Henry. And we'll get it all done before the new addition. So we're not just a family, but legal. Names and everything."

She cupped his face with her hands, studying his face very seriously. "That's a lovely sentiment, but I hope you know we don't need names for that."

"No, but it'll be nice. It'll be official. A baby. Our baby. Our *family*." He shook his head. Too bowled over to say much more. "I don't know how…"

"I know you think we saved you, but you were exactly what we needed, too." She pressed a kiss to his mouth. "We're all exactly where we're supposed to be. All four of us."

Exactly where he was supposed to be. Finally.

* * * * *

WE HOPE YOU ENJOYED
THIS BOOK FROM
✦ HARLEQUIN

INTRIGUE

Seek thrills. Solve crimes. Justice served.

Dive into action-packed stories that will keep you
on the edge of your seat. Solve the crime
and deliver justice at all costs.

6 NEW BOOKS AVAILABLE EVERY MONTH!

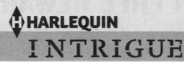

Get 4 FREE REWARDS!

We'll send you 2 FREE Books
plus 2 FREE Mystery Gifts.

Harlequin Intrigue books are action-packed stories that will keep you on the edge of your seat. Solve the crime and deliver justice at all costs.

FREE Value Over **$20**

Love Harlequin romance?

DISCOVER.

Be the first to find out about promotions, news and exclusive content!

f Facebook.com/HarlequinBooks

𝕏 Twitter.com/HarlequinBooks

◉ Instagram.com/HarlequinBooks

℗ Pinterest.com/HarlequinBooks

ReaderService.com

EXPLORE.

Sign up for the Harlequin e-newsletter and download a free book from any series at **TryHarlequin.com**

CONNECT.

Join our Harlequin community to share your thoughts and connect with other romance readers!
Facebook.com/groups/HarlequinConnection